The Wonder Wig

The Wonder Wig

❖

Dr. Shon Shree Lewis

Copyright © 2021 by Dr. Shon Shree Lewis.

ISBN:	Softcover	978-1-6641-4936-6
	eBook	978-1-6641-4937-3

All rights reserved. No part of this book may be reproduced or transmitted in any form or by any means, electronic or mechanical, including photocopying, recording, or by any information storage and retrieval system, without permission in writing from the copyright owner.

This is a work of fiction. Names, characters, places and incidents either are the product of the author's imagination or are used fictitiously, and any resemblance to any actual persons, living or dead, events, or locales is entirely coincidental.

Any people depicted in stock imagery provided by Getty Images are models, and such images are being used for illustrative purposes only.
Certain stock imagery © Getty Images.

Print information available on the last page.

Rev. date: 12/29/2020

To order additional copies of this book, contact:
Xlibris
844-714-8691
www.Xlibris.com
Orders@Xlibris.com
815609

Contents

My Book Characters vii
Chapter 1   Brooke's Identity Crisis 1
Chapter 2   Brooke's New Home 27
Chapter 3   The Battle of the Hair 46
Chapter 4   The Mysterious Wonder Wig 55
Chapter 5   Brooke's Awareness to Alopecia 62
Chapter 6   "Wiggin It"- The Beauty Contest 72
Chapter 7   The Wonder Wig Revealed 101

About the Author 121

My Book Characters

Main Character – Brooke Bell

Brooke's Dad – Craig Bell

Brooke's Mom – Barb Bell

Dale Bell – Brooke's Paternal Grandfather

Lucy Bell – Brooke's Paternal Grandmother

Pam – Brooke's Aunt

Jill – Pam's Daughter

Ms. Wright – Brooke's Schoolteacher

William – Brooke's boy interest

Ruth – Brooke's Friend

CHAPTER 1

Brooke's Identity Crisis

Once upon a time, there was a country family that lived in Arkansas; a man named Craig Bell, his wife named Barb, and their only child, a little girl named Brooke. Craig and Barb worked outside of the house all the time. Craig worked as a construction worker, and Barb at her hair salon called, *That Look*, and they would only have quality time together, and with their daughter, mostly on weekends. So many times, starting at the age of seven, Brooke's yellow bus would drop her off at the home of her father's parents until her mother would pick her up later in the evening, after 7:00 p.m., to take her home.

Brooke's grandmother's name was Lucy, and her grandfather, Dale. She loved her grandparents dearly because, they gave her the time and care she always longed for from her parents. She also liked being at their home because, she felt safe and she would see her aunt Pam and her cousin Jill, who was just two years older than her, and they would have fun playing with their grandmother Lucy's makeup glam on her vanity dresser in her powder room. So Brooke never felt lonely around them. However, when she would be at home with her parents, after breakfast, lunch, dinner, and short family time, Brooke often felt lonely because many times her parents would be so tired from their workplaces, and although their family time together was fun, it was short, and Brooke resented that about her parents. She was the only child, and had no sister or brother to talk to or play toy dolls and trucks with together. This made her very sad. Sometimes Brooke's mother would try to accommodate her loneliness, by taking her on a shopping spree to buy Brooke pretty dresses and fashion jewelry. This made Brooke happy for a while, but she still felt discontent because, her parents were hardly together for family time and she had no siblings.

3

There would be times when her grandmother Lucy would give Brooke and her parents a surprise visit, and would bring Brooke some of the most beautiful Barbie dolls of all races, with long extravagant hair, and Brooke adored her Barbie dolls and always felt more special when her grandmother Lucy was around her. Because she always treated Brooke like a little princess. Brooke would oftentimes compare the perm hair on her head, with her Barbie dolls. Her hair was so short compared with her dolls, and she didn't understand why she always had short black hair, and why her hair wasn't long and pretty like her Barbie dolls, or like her grandmother Lucy's. Brooke pondered this in her heart at a young age. Something Brooke also noticed was, her mom also had short hair, but she always saw her mom wear different beautiful wigs she simply adored and thought were stunning. But, Brooke knew she was too young to wear them.

One day, at the age of ten, Brooke wanted to impress a boy she liked at school, so she sneaked one of her mom's wigs to school. This wig was a dazzling shoulder-length wavy brownish-red hair. Mostly everybody in school was staring at Brooke and admiring her hair, even the young boy Brooke liked in school. Then suddenly, when Brooke dropped one of her school notebooks, her wig fell off her head, and a lot of the students in her school began to laugh at her. Brooke felt so ashamed. She tried to hold back her tears, and she noticed the boy she liked was looking at her, but he politely picked up her notebook, handed it to her, and walked away. Brooke began to cry.

She ran in the school hallway, furious, disappearing into the girls' bathroom, hiding for one hour. Then she fixed her wig, wiped her tears, while sniffling on a Kleenex from the bathroom counter. When she finally heard the school bell ring for the end of the school day, she quickly ran out of the bathroom, and as she was walking toward the school door to catch her school bus, her teacher Ms. Wright said, "Brooke, darling, where were you? What's wrong?"

Brooke shamefully looked at her teacher and said, "I am sorry, Ms. Wright, I wasn't feeling well."

Ms. Wright replied with empathy and said, "I hope you feel better, we will talk hopefully tomorrow, and I am going to give your parents a call this evening."

Brooke shook her head and said, "No, Ms. Wright, I am fine!" Then Brooke ran toward the school doors to catch her bus.

Afterward, Ms. Wright did use her cell phone and called Brooke's Mom at the hair salon, telling her, Brooke was missing for a while from class, saying she didn't feel well. Brooke's mom was worried and not happy about the phone call, but she had clients' hair to style, and could not think about Brooke at the time. Barb definitely was determined to find out what happened with her daughter later.

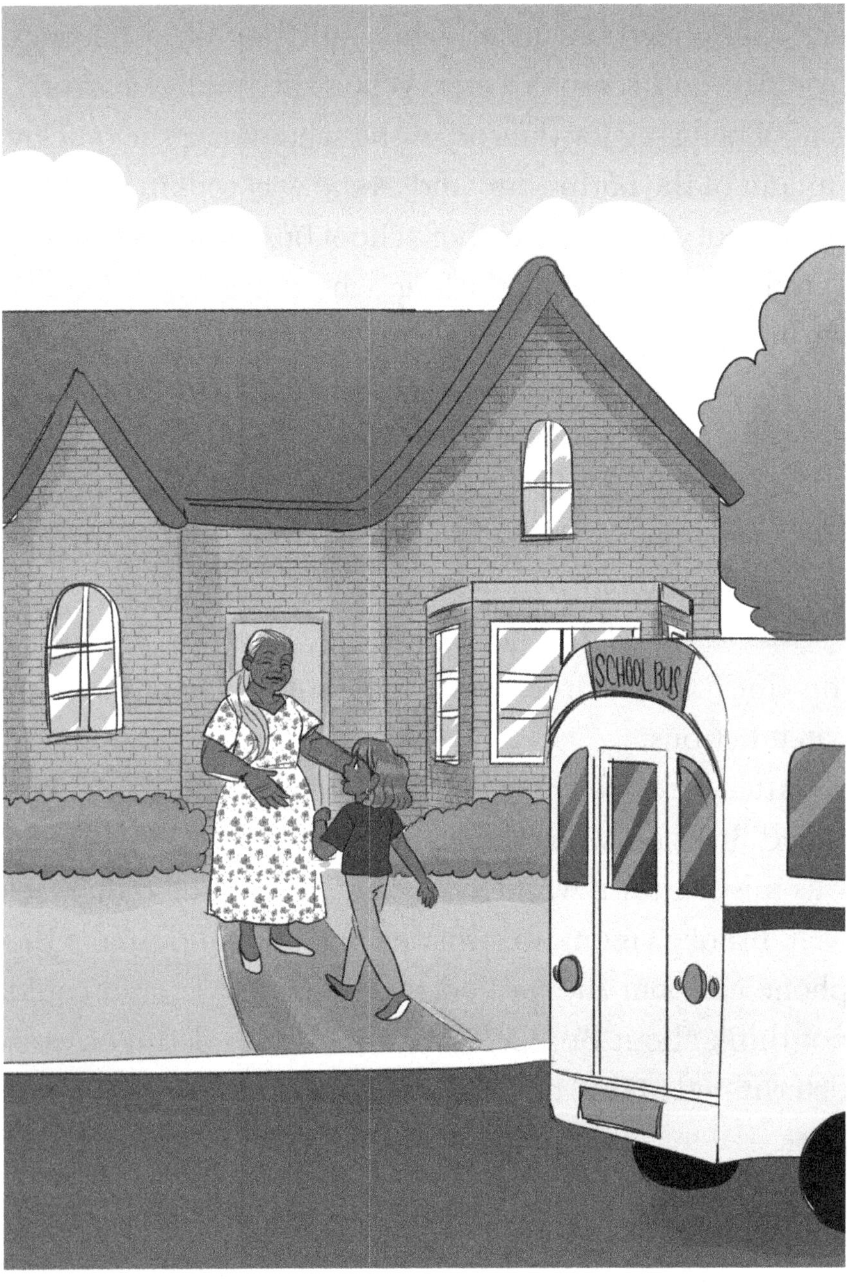
SCHOOL BUS

Meanwhile, Brooke got to her grandparents' house, and her grandmother Lucy was astonished to see the wig Brooke was wearing, as she walked up to her house door from her school bus. Brooke knew her grandmother was staring at her. She gave her grandmother Lucy a half grin walking in her house. Brooke could smell some good ole fried chicken, and buttered rice cooking on her grandmother Lucy's stove.

As Brooke put her book bag on her grandmother Lucy's living room floor, at the corner, Brooke walked to her grandmother, hugged her, and said sorrowfully, "Granny Lu, I had a bad day today at school."

Brooke's grandmother looked at her sympathetically, rubbed her face cheek, and said, "Sit down baby, tell me what happened, something wrong with your hair?"

Brooke sat down with her grandmother on her gray leather sofa. Brooke then said tearfully, "I took one of Mom's wigs from home to wear to school today so I can look prettier, and my wig fell off in front of my class friends and other students, and I was so embarrassed, I ran to the girls' bathroom and cried. until I heard the school bell ring. Then I left the school bathroom, and my teacher Ms. Wright saw me, and was wondering why I was missing in class, and I told her I was sick, and she said she was going to call Mom, and I feel terrible." Brooke then laid her face on her grandmother's shoulders and weeped.

Grandma Lucy held her granddaughter with compassion, wiping her tears with a Kleenex from her glass table, and she said, "Baby, it will be okay, you stop that crying." Then she asked, "Why did you feel you needed to wear a wig to look beautiful?"

Brooke sniffed and wiped her nose with her Kleenex and said, "I just wanted to look beautiful, Granny Lu, and Mom has so many wigs, I thought I would try on one to look more pretty for school, because my hair is so short, and not pretty like the other girls in school."

"I see," Grandma Lucy said, smiling with a gazed look. Then Grandma Lucy said, "Brooke, you are very beautiful, and a wig cannot make you more beautiful than you were born to be." Brooke looked into her grandmother's eyes, listening with sincerity to her words, and Brooke's eyes swelled again with tears.

Brooke said, "But my hair is so short and not pretty like yours, Granny Lu."

"Stop that!" Grandmother Lucy said with firmness.

Brooke continued to say, "Then when my wig fell off at school, some of the students laughed at me, and I was so embarrassed when William handed me my notebook, and he walked away like he felt sorry for me. I just wanted to die, Granny."

"William—is he a boy crush you have?" Brooke looked away from her grandmother, smirking as she sniffled.

Her grandmother Lucy said, grinning, "Aha, so this is why you wore the wig, hmmm, young lady?"

Brooke looked up slowly at her grandmother and said slowly, "Yes. He's cute, Granny Lu, and I wanted to look pretty for him, and now I don't know if he thinks I am the worst girl in the world, or if he will ever want to be my friend." Brooke began to weep again, mumbling to her grandmother about feeling bad about her day.

Her grandmother Lucy replied, "Brooke, look at me, I understand you wanted to look nice for yourself and for this boy William, but you have to be happy with how God made you first, and you are already beautiful, whether you have short or long hair, wig or no wig. Also, if you did not ask your mother to wear her wig darling, that means you stole it, and that was wrong baby, and you will need to explain to your mother and apologize to her later. Do you understand?"

Brooke looked at her grandmother with respect and said, "Yes, Granny Lu."

Then her grandmother said to Brooke, "You remember to always love who you are first, before you expect anyone else to like and love you. You are a sweet little girl and someday, will be a fine young woman. Don't ever let your hair define who you are. It is who you are as a person, your morals of behaving right, and being kind to others, that make you a special and beautiful person. Also remember, you are loved by your parents, and Papa and I love you dearly, and that is what matters." Brooke nodded, to acknowledge she was listening to her grandmother.

Suddenly, Brooke's grandpa Dale walked in the living room. He was carrying a newspaper and going to his favorite black leather recliner chair, looking at Brooke wiping her eyes, and her grandfather said, "What's wrong with Grandpa's baby?"

Grandma Lucy raised Brooke's head from her shoulder as Brooke sniffled and dried her eyes with Kleenex. Brooke smiled, as she fixed her wig and looked at her grandpa and said, "Hi Papa, I am okay."

Grandma Lucy says to her husband Grandpa Dale, "She's fine, honey."

Grandpa Dale says to Brooke, "Give your old grandpa a hug."

Brooke grinned, and ran to her grandpa and gave him a tight hug. He touches her wig and said with amusement, "What's this?"

Brooke said, chuckling and shrugging, "A new experiment."

Both her grandparents laughed with joy. Then Grandpa Dale handed Brooke a piece of peppermint candy. Brooke took the candy and kissed her grandpa Dale on his face cheek and said, "Thanks Papa."

Grandma Lucy smiled, and said to Brooke, "Go wash your hands in the bathroom and come in the kitchen with me so we can get dinner ready, baby."

Brooke said, "Okay, Grandma Lu."

After Brooke had spent a nice time having dinner with her grandparents, and watching a game show on television, of matching store items with right prices, Brooke realized it was almost time for her mom to arrive to pick her up from her grandparents. Then Brooke tried to remove the wig in front of her grandma Lu after dinner, but her grandma Lu insisted she keep the wig on, until Brooke's mom arrived to pick her up to take her home.

Finally, Brooke's mother arrived after 7:00 p.m. to pick up Brooke from her grandmother's house. As Brooke's mother, Barb, walked into the living room of Brooke's grandmother, she looked at Brooke, shocked, recognizing her wig on her daughter. Barb was surprised and upset because, Brooke's teacher called her on the phone, and it did not make sense, until she saw Brooke wearing her wig.

"Hi Grandma Lucy," Barb said respectfully, as she hugged her. Then Barb said hello to Grandpa Dale, and he replied, "Hi darling."

Grandmother Lucy replied to Barb, "Hey baby, how was work?"

"It was okay, busy as usual," said Barb. Brooke was looking hesitantly at her mom, as her mom gave her a puzzled stare. Grandma Lucy noticed both of them looking at each other, anticipating; Brooke feeling ashamed.

Barb walked over to Brooke and touched her wig and said, "So young lady, what is this, my wig? Your teacher called me today and said you were sick, but it doesn't look like it to me."

"Mom, I'm sorry, I can explain," Brooke said sadly.

Grandma Lucy said to Barb, "Don't be too rough on her Barb."

Barb smiled sarcastically at Grandma Lucy and said, "I appreciate you and Papa taking care of her while me and her dad are at work, but I must teach her not to steal." Brooke looked at her mom sadly, and really dreaded leaving her grandparents' house. After Brooke hugged her grandfather and grandmother, she and her mom said their goodbyes for the day, and walked to Barb's gold Chevy truck. There was silence in Brooke's mother truck, as they were traveling home. Once they got home in fifteen minutes, it was just Brooke and her mom at home, because Brooke's dad would not get home from work until after 8:00 p.m.

So Brooke's Mom said to Brooke, "You put your book bag away in your room, take off my wig, bring it to me, and let's talk about today, before you do your homework."

Brooke replied, "I did my homework at Granny Lu's house."

After Brooke walked into her home's dining room where her mom was sitting, drinking a cup of tea, Brooke's mom looked at her with disappointment, as Brooke handed her mom the wig that belonged to her. Then Brooke sat at one of her mom's dining room chairs, looking apprehensive at her mom.

Her mom looking serious, asked, "Now what is the meaning of you taking my wig to wear to school today and missing class?"

Brooke, with eyes looking ashamed at the dining room table, said, "Mom, I don't like my hair, it's too short, and you always wear wigs to look prettier, and I wanted to look prettier today at school, and your wig fell off my head, and kids laughed at me, so I sat in the school bathroom the last hour of school because I was embarrassed." Brooke's eyes began to show her tears.

Barb, her mom, looked at her with some compassion but said, "Baby, I understand you like wigs as I do, but you could have asked me instead of sneaking into my room to take it. When you wear wigs, you have to wear hair pins to keep the wig on your head to avoid it falling. Anyway, it sounds like you were trying to impress someone. Were you?"

Brooke did not feel comfortable talking to her mom about boys like she did her Grandma Lu.

Brooke replied defiantly, "I don't want to talk about it."

"What do you mean you don't want to talk about it?" Brooke's mom asked. Brooke remained silent.

Feeling frustrated, Barb then said to Brooke, "Because you took my wig without my permission, I have to discipline you darling, to teach you not to take things without a person's permission. So there will be no recreational activities outside of the house and no television for a week."

Brooke's eyes began to tear up. She was so upset. Then she asked, "What about at Grandma Lu and Papa Dale's house?"

Her mom replied firmly, "I can't control what you do there, but when you get home, there will be no television or dessert after your dinners here for a week."

"I said I am sorry Mom," Brooke said with remorse.

Barb responded, "Thank you, I love you, but I have to show you tough love. One day you will be old enough to wear a wig, but right now, you are too young Brooke."

Brooke looked at her mom, trying to honor her, but she felt misunderstood and hurt inside her heart about her mom's punishment. Just as her mom finished talking, Brooke's dad walked in from work.

"Hello," he said tiredly, walking in the door with muddy construction clothes and boots.

Barb looked up at her husband and said, "Hey baby, how was work?"

Craig, her husband said, "The usual. Thank God, not much rain today,

while I was finishing building the sidewalk for that new clothing store I was telling you about." Craig then noticed one of Barb's wigs on the dining room table and looked over at his daughter who looked troubled and upset.

Craig then said, "What's wrong with my baby?" Brooke looked at her dad, her eyes swelling up with tears, and she ran to her dad to embrace him, and wept in his arms. Barb looked annoyed at Brooke, as she was looking for her father's sympathy.

Brooke's father rubbed his daughter's shoulders and face, and he raised her face to look at him, and he asked, "What's wrong? What happened today?"

Brooke, barely able to speak, stuttered to explain to her dad what happened with her in school, and how her mom punished her.

Barb tried to interrupt by saying, "Craig, she stole one of my wigs today, probably to impress some ugly boy crush she has."

Brooke looked at her mom with anger and interrupted her and shouted, "Dad, I left class because I wore one of Mom's wigs to school, and it fell off, and the kids at school laughed at me!" Brooke then hugged her dad again as she cried in his arms. Barb shook her head, looking angry.

Brooke's dad asked Barb, "What did you do about it?"

Barb said, "Craig, I had a good talk with her, and I told her she is on punishment for a week, no television or dessert."

Brooke's dad looked at Barb dumbfounded and said, "I think that is too harsh. Let's go talk about this in a few minutes Barb."

Barb said aggressively, "There is nothing to talk about Craig! I told you how I disciplined her." Brooke sniffled and began to dry her eyes with her hands, as she looked hopeful at her dad defending her.

Her dad began to argue with her mom, saying, "Barb, you should have talked with me first, before you made this decision. She obviously is hurting, and it was an innocent mistake!"

"Craig! Why are you disrespecting my authority as her mother?" Barb yelled.

Brooke's dad looked at his daughter and said with kindness, "Baby, let me and your mother talk. You will be okay. Go to your room, and I will be in there to talk to you and say good night soon." Then, Brooke's dad kissed her on her face cheek.

Brooke smiled and said, "Okay Daddy." Brooke felt a lot better, and walked into her bedroom and closed her bedroom door, standing by her door to try to listen to her parents argue. Because her parents walked into their bedroom to talk, she could not hear them. So Brooke sat on her bed looking at her homework until she fell asleep.

Meanwhile, Barb and Craig were arguing quietly.

Craig said, "Barb, I don't agree with Brooke stealing, you know how I feel about people who steal. However, she is just a kid, trying to become a better person. Maybe because she feels insecure, and with all the gorgeous wigs you have in this house, she was bound to try one at some time. All I am saying Barb is, give her a break." Barb began to look guilty and quieted herself, and began to think about what her husband Craig was saying.

Barb then said, "I don't want my baby looking older than what she is, because she is trying to impress some boy she has a crush on. She is too young Craig."

Craig looked at his wife with sympathy and said, "Our baby is growing up, and we have to let her make mistakes, and when she does, we must find out why she made a bad choice, before we discipline her. She may just need a good talking to. That's what my parents taught me when they raised me."

Barb replied, "Well, your parents did not seem too concerned when I got to their house to pick up Brooke."

Craig said, "Mom and Dad don't make big deals about that kind of stuff, Barb. Brooke is a good kid, and they know that." Barb felt condemned about her response to her daughter, and she reminisced about her younger days of trying on her mother's wigs, to try to understand

Brooke's feelings. But she did not like her trying to grow up too fast, and that was what concerned her.

Craig said to Barb, "Let me go talk with Brooke before my dinner with you, and remind her what is right and wrong, and comfort her with my words to talk to us if she ever feels bad or concerned about anything."

"So what about my punishment to her?" Barb asked with curiosity, to see if her husband was going to try to change her method of discipline.

Craig paused and said to Barb, "I think one day is enough punishment, not a whole week. If she does this again, God forbid, then a week would be reasonable to me."

Barb looked upset and said, "Craig, I don't agree, but I will respect your feelings on this matter, but in the future, you and I need to compromise, and not show Brooke that we are divided with our disciplining her, or she will lose respect for us and try to play us against each other, and I am not having that."

Craig listened to his wife Barb with respect and said, "I hear you, and okay, let's work on that together." Brooke woke up, as she heard her dad knock lightly on her bedroom door. Brooke sat up and yawned, wiping her eyes to focus her attention to her dad. Her father smiled, walked toward her, and sat on the recliner in her room.

"Hi Daddy," Brooke said, smiling. Barb walked toward Brooke's bedroom and stood in the doorway of her room to listen to their conversation.

Brooke's father said to her with tenderness, "Brooke, your mother and I talked about what happened with you today. First, I want to say you are beautiful baby, and no wig can ever make you look better than you already are. You are our princess, and you have to believe that. I also don't want you trying to impress any boy, who is not good enough, if he can't like you for who you are. So never make a bad choice, just to impress or be accepted by others. Stealing your mother's wig was not right baby. Do you get that?"

Brooke looked at her daddy with honor and said, "Yes Daddy." Brooke also glanced at her mother who was standing by her bedroom door, looking seriously at her with her arms folded.

Brooke's father continued to say, "Because you stole your mother's wig and missed some of your classroom time, you will have a consequence for your bad choice. However, you are only grounded for a day, not a week." Brooke smirked, looking happy.

Her mom then said harshly, "I agree with your father, and this is to teach you a lesson not to steal. So don't let it happen again because if this happens again, you will be punished for a longer period, and we are not changing it. You understand, Brooke?"

Brooke responded slowly, looking at her mom with bitterness, "Yes Mom."

Brooke's father said, "All right my princess, time for you to go to bed." He kissed her face cheek and said, "Good night."

Brooke said, "Good night Daddy."

Brooke's mom looked at her and said, "Good night Brooke."

Brooke, feeling some resentment toward her mom, said, "Good night."

Her parents walked out of her room and slightly closed her bedroom door. Brooke felt good about her dad's words to her, but she was still angry with her mom because Brooke believed it was her dad who defended her and changed her punishment. Brooke held resentment in her heart toward her mom from that day because she could not understand why her mom would not spend the time she wanted with her, to show her fashion and hair styling like her grandmother Lu would at times.

Although Brooke would miss her dad, she wanted badly to live with his parents,(her grandparents), because she felt more loved there and knew her dad would visit her at his parents' house regularly if she moved with his parents. Also, Brooke would oftentimes see her aunt Pam and her daughter named Jill, who was two years older than Brooke, stop by her grandparents' home. Brooke enjoyed spending time with her aunt Pam, especially her cousin Jill, whom she loved spending television and play time with, using their grandmother's hair and makeup from her glam bag on her dresser. Brooke also wanted her freedom to wear what she wanted, without her mom punishing her and stopping her from expressing herself with fashion, so Brooke plotted to find a way to move away from her parents, to go live with her grandparents.

A week later, Brooke decided to try to ask her parents if she could live with her grandparents for the summer. Although Brooke knew her father would be completely fine with the idea of his daughter spending the summer with his parents, Brooke's mom was not because, she feared Brooke getting into more trouble with school or boys away from her discipline.

So the day Brooke asked her mom could she spend a summer with her grandparents, Barb said, "No."

Brooke asked, "Why Mom?"

Then Brooke's mom said, "I forbid you to live with your grandparents, so you can get away with bad behavior. I simply won't have it!"

Brooke, in anger and tears, shouted boldly, "Why? I don't see you and Dad hardly until the end of the day and weekends, and I am the only child with no one to talk to or play toys with my age. I am tired of being by myself. I want to spend the summer with Grandma Lucy and Grandpa. If I can't stay with them for the summer, I am running away!"

Suddenly, Brooke's dad walked into the living room, hearing the argument and asked Barb, "Now what's going on with you and Brooke?"

Barb yelled, "This little girl is talking about she going to run away if we don't let her move in with your parents for the summer. Absolutely not!"

Brooke replied, "Daddy, I love you and Mom, but I want to stay with Grandma Lu and Papa for the summer and see Aunt Pam and Jill. I have more fun there since I don't have any siblings."

Brooke's father said, "Barb, I don't see anything wrong with her staying by my parents for the summer. She needs a change of scenery, and she is right, she doesn't have anyone to play her toys with when she gets home. It's just us, and she may get lonely at times as a child, not having another child around her." Brooke adored her dad and was so happy he was defending her again, and considering how she felt.

Barb said, "Craig, don't you see, she is too young to be gone for a whole summer. Your parents will not be able to keep up with all the female changes that she will be experiencing this summer."

Craig argued back and said, "We can check on her every day, that won't change."

Barb said, "I am not going to be stopping over there every day, if she is not going to be home with us!" Brooke got so furious listening to her mom complain and go against her dad. Then Brooke suddenly, ran out of the living room and left the house, heading toward her grandparents' house.

Barb shouted, "Brooke, where are you going?" Craig, feeling upset, followed Barb toward their house front door, trying to see where Brooke was running, but she disappeared so quickly from their sight. Brooke knew a shortcut to run toward her grandparents' home that was fifteen minutes away.

Craig yelled at Barb and said, "Now you see what you have done? She is probably going to Mom and Dad's house. Let me call them and stop over there."

Barb said, "I am going too."

Craig said, "Barb, no! Brooke does not want to see you right now. Let me handle this, and I will let you know what happens, and you can talk to her another time."

Barb began to cry and say, "Craig, I don't know what to do with her."

Craig walked over to his wife and hugged her, saying, "Everything will be all right. You just sit and relax. Let me handle this. She will be fine at my parents' house for as long as she needs to stay." On his cell phone, Craig called his parents' house as he rushed out of his house toward his burgundy Chevy truck.

In a short time, Brooke, almost out of breath, finally made it to her grandparents' house. Already expecting Brooke from her son's phone call, Grandma Lu let Brooke in her house with a warm hug yet acting surprised.

Grandma Lu then kindly asked, "What are you doing here young lady, and how did you get here?"

Brooke, gasping for air from running from her parents' house, said, "Grandma Lu, I want to stay with you and Papa."

"Why, what happened?" Grandma Lu asked.

"Mom is mean, and I am lonely at home. I have fun here with you and Papa because, you are always home, and when Aunt Pam stops by, I have fun with Cousin Jill," Brooke replied. Grandma Lu gave a blank stare to

Brooke because, she understood how Brooke felt, but did not want her upsetting her parents.

Suddenly, Brooke heard a truck pull up outside her grandparents' house, and she panicked and looked through her grandparents' window and saw her dad's truck.

Brooke said, "Grandma Lu, I will talk to Daddy if he is by himself, but I will not talk to Mom."

"You just calm yourself," Grandma Lu said. "Take a cookie from my cookie jar." Brooke walked over to Grandma Lu's kitchen to get a cookie from the cookie jar and walked back into her grandparents' living room, where her Grandma Lu was walking toward her door to let her son Craig in her house. Brooke noticed her dad was by himself, and she felt better. Lucy, smiling, opened her front house door and let her son Craig in the house.

"Hi Mama," Craig said happily.

After Lucy closed her door, she hugged her son with such joy and said, "Hi son, so good to see you, and not just hear your voice over the phone." Craig saw his daughter Brooke eating a cookie as they looked at each other.

Brooke ran to her dad and cried, saying, "Daddy, I am sorry I ran away. Please don't punish me. Can I please live here for the summer, please?"

Then Dale walked out of the sitting room and looked over at his son, surprised and happy to see him.

"Hey Dad!" Craig said with respect, grinning.

"Hey Craig. What brings you here son?" Dale said, as he hugged his son.

Craig said jokingly, "Just your little princess Brooke."

Craig's dad said with humor, "I wonder if that wig had anything to do with this."

Craig nodded yes to his dad. Brooke looking bashful, looked at both of them, and then at Grandma Lu, who was smiling, and offering her son some tea or bottled water.

"No Mama, I'm fine, thank you," Craig said graciously.

Suddenly, Dale heard his house phone ring. He looked at the caller ID and saw it was Barb calling. Craig's dad said, "Craig, it's your wife. Should I answer?"

Craig said, "No Dad, I told her I will talk to her later." Then Craig said to his parents, Mama and Dad, I am so sorry to inconvenience you this way, but Brooke and I need to talk to you and explain what is happening with her." Brooke looked at her dad, anticipating what he might say that will support her living with them for the summer starting that week.

Her dad said, "Brooke spoke her concerns to me and her mother today, and they make sense to me. I feel bad I am not home enough when I get home from work, and that her mom has to pick her up so late, weekly from your house, not to mention she has no siblings. So although her mom and I disagreed, I support how our daughter is feeling. Would you be okay with her living with you two for the summer, and we will check on her as much as we can?" Brooke looked at her grandparents nervously, hoping they would say yes.

Grandpa Dale responded, "We don't mind our little plum staying here, but she hasn't asked us."

Craig looked at his daughter and said, "Brooke?"

Brooke looked at her dad and her grandparents and said humbly, "I love Mom and Dad, I don't understand Mom like Dad, and I will miss them, but can I stay here for the summer because I like being around you and Aunt Pam and Jill?"

Smiling, Grandma Lu grabbed Brooke's chin and said, "You most certainly can!"

Grandpa Dale said happily, "It is official."

Brooke jumped for joy then hugged her dad and grandparents, saying, "Thank you! Thank you! Thank you!"

Craig nodded, confirming the agreement with his approval.

Dale then asked his son Craig, "What about Barb?" Craig looked at his father and said, "She's not going to like it, but I will talk to her, and she will adjust."

"Well, tomorrow I will bring some of your things over since it is Saturday and I don't have to work. Hopefully, your mom can stop by after work," says Brooke's Dad.

"Okay Daddy," Brooke said cheerfully.

Grandma Lu said, "Speaking of your sister Pam, she's supposed to be stopping by tomorrow with Jill, and maybe Jill can spend a night here with Brooke."

Brooke's dad says, "Good, I need to talk to my sister anyway. I will let Barb know." Craig said his goodbyes to his parents, hugged his daughter, and dialed his wife's cell phone as he was walking out of his parents' house.

"Hello," Craig said to Barb by phone.

"Where is my baby?" Barb was heard saying on the speaker of the phone, as Craig closed his parents' house door.

Chapter 2

Brooke's New Home

It was Saturday, and Brooke was thrilled to be living with her grandparents. Her hope was to stay with them and not to return to her parent's home because, she felt so much love and attention at her grandparent's home, and had her best times with her grandparents. She also knew she would see her dad all the time, so that comforted her as well. Brooke always had the guest room her grandparents had available for her and Jill to use.

Later that morning, Aunt Pam and Jill arrived during breakfast. Brooke was so happy to see her aunt Pam. She admired her beauty and fashion because she wore dazzling clothes and gorgeous hairstyles, whether it was her hair, a wig, or a weave.

Aunt Pam and Jill walked to Grandma Lu's breakfast island in her kitchen. Jill pushed back her eyeglasses to her face, excited to have the delectable food Grandma Lu had on the counter. Aunt Pam and Jill could see golden brown pancakes stacked on a white marble plate with bacon and orange juice set on the counter.

Cheerfully, Grandma Lu said, "Hey babies!" Brooke looked thrilled. Pam hugged her mother and Brooke.

Jill smiled at Brooke and said, "Hi Brooke."

Brooke got up from her chair and said, "Hey Jill, you staying for the weekend?"

Brooke's aunt Pam said, "Sure, that is why I brought her, and are you staying too?"

Brooke's Grandma Lu said to her aunt Pam, "She is actually staying for the summer. Long story. I will explain to you. Have a seat Pam."

So Pam was delighted to enjoy a hearty meal with her mom Lucy, her daughter Jill, and her niece Brooke that day.

"Can Jill and I go outside and play rope, Grandma Lu?" Brooke asked. Jill was looking anxious to go play rope with her cousin.

Grandma Lu said, "Yes, you girls wash your hands and stay in front of the house, where we can see you." Jill looked at her mom Pam, and she nodded to her, giving her the okay to go play outside with Brooke.

Brooke and Jill ran eagerly to the kitchen sink to wash their hands, and they chuckled as they headed for Grandma Lu's front door to leave her house and go on the sidewalk with a jump rope Brooke grabbed from Grandma Lu's porch.

Pam smiled at her mother and said, "Those girls."

Her mother Lucy smiled and said, "Yes, they are happy girls."

"So, Mom, what is going on with my brother Craig and him letting Brooke live with you for the summer? Did him and Barb have a fight?"

Her mother shook her head, looking with amusement, and said, "Well, sort of because, Brooke has been having a hard time with Barb not understanding Brooke being so focused on her appearance these days. Craig is sympathetic, while Barb is upset and feels scared for Brooke's level of maturity, of wanting to look more grown-up. Brooke had the nerve to wear one of Barb's brownish red wigs to school." Lucy began to giggle to herself.

"No . . . Mother, are you for real?" Pam asked with humor.

"Yes girl," her mother Lucy said, and she laughed louder.

Pam took a gulp of her orange juice and said, "I do think Barb is being a little too hard on Brooke. I talk to Jill all the time about hair and fashion, and I let her play with some of my wigs at home just so she can learn how to cherish other styles of beauty. Even though she has long hair from your side of the family, Mom, Jill likes the wigs but doesn't have much interest in them. She likes my makeup more. I let her try it every now and then, but I don't let her wear it outside the house."

"Yes, Barb doesn't understand how to let loose on Brooke and have fun with her as she teaches her fashion the same way I taught you when I used to work at my hair salon before I retired years ago," Lucy said to her daughter Pam.

"Hmmm, well, I hope this arrangement works with Brooke and you, and maybe Barb will come to her senses and stop being so hard on this girl. Anyway, I must call my brother Craig soon and make sure he is okay, considering the changes their household just gone through with Brooke temporarily being gone."

Lucy replied, "Yeah, check on your brother, but don't get in the middle of him and Barb's quarrel."

"I won't Mother," Pam replied.

Half an hour had passed as Lucy and Pam continued to laugh and talk hair talk and about hair salon events. Then Lucy and Pam could hear Brooke's and Jill's laughter near the house. Pam walked to the living room window to check on them. They were cheerfully jumping rope, taking turns with the jump rope. Suddenly, Pam began to see raindrops falling outside on the grass.

Pam said, "Let me get the girls, Mom. It is starting to rain."

Lucy heard some thunder. Before Pam went outside, Brooke and Jill ran in the house, energetic and laughing about the rain they just escaped from outdoors.

Grandma Lu said to her granddaughters, "Did you girls get your clothes too wet from the rain? Come here, let me see."

Pam was looking at the girls smiling, and Jill said, "No Grandma Lu, we are good, just my glasses are foggy."

Brooke smirked and said, "I'm a little damp because Jill ran in the house before me." Jill began to laugh.

Pam and her mother Lucy smiled. Then Pam said, "Well Jill, let's go. I have to get to the hair salon before these clients show up there soon."

Brooke began to look sad and said, "Aunt Pam, does she have to go?"

Aunt Pam said, "I'm sorry baby, yes. I need her to help clean up, and she gets a little allowance for helping me. But I will bring her back tonight." Brooke looks grieved. Aunt Pam then said, "Brooke, how about you come along with us for the day?"

Brooke's countenance changed from sad to geeked, and she said, "Can I? Can I, Grandma Lu?" Jill was smiling.

Grandma Lu looked into her granddaughter's eyes and could see the curiosity and the eagerness to go be with her aunt and cousin, and she replied, "Yes baby, you can go hang out with your aunt Pam and cousin Jill, and she will have to bring you and Jill back after work, so right now, go get changed into one of your T-shirts and jeans. You be sure you behave yourself in front of those customers."

"Yes Grandma Lu, I promise I will be good," said Brooke.

Then Brooke immediately, dashed to the guest room, to change her clothing. Afterward, she walked back into the living room where Grandma Lu, Aunt Pam, and Jill were talking and waiting for her.

"Okay Mom, let us get going. Love you Mom," Pam said.

Brooke and Jill hugged their Grandma Lu, and Grandma Lu said to her daughter Pam, "Love you too Pam, and the baby girls."

Pam walked out of her mom's house with the girls, and as she got into her blue Chevy pickup truck, the girls turned around to look at their grandmother. Grandma Lu waved happily at all of them as Pam drove away. Grandma Lu smiled and closed her house door and prepared to rest in her recliner chair. She was at peace and happy about Brooke getting some quality family time with Pam, and she was looking forward to hearing later how their day had been.

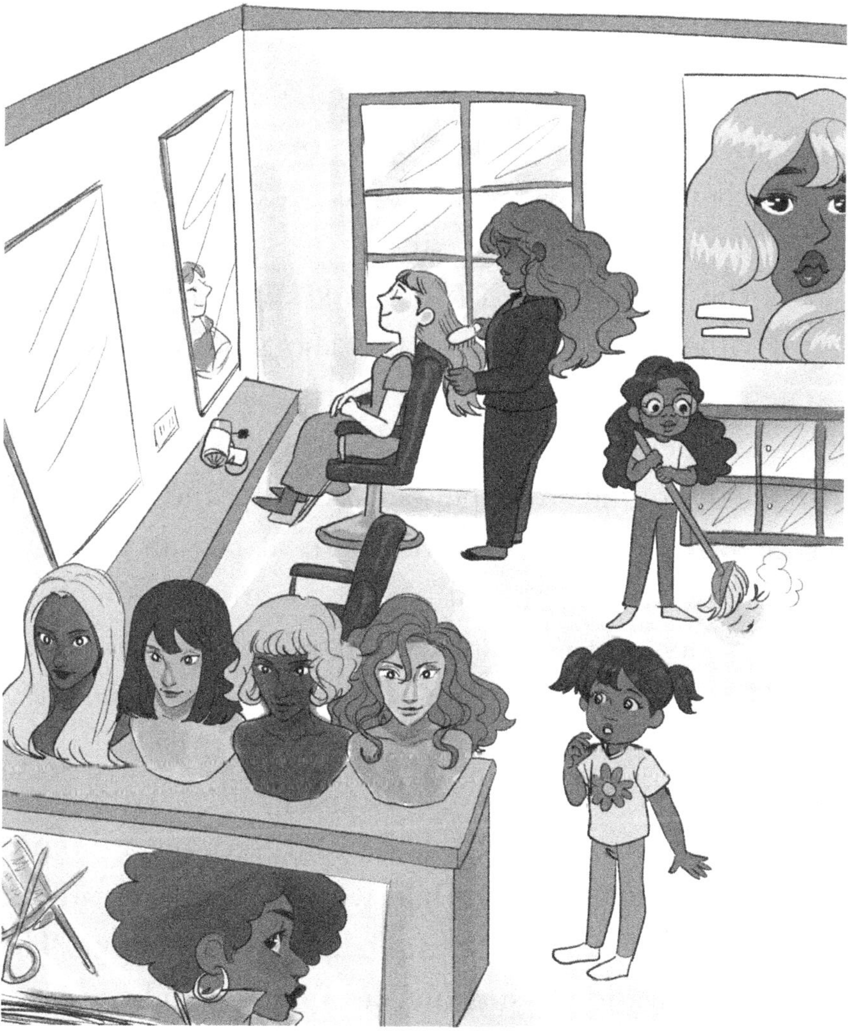

Aunt Pam finally arrived at her hair salon with her daughter Jill and her niece Brooke, and began to show Brooke the variety of fashion of wigs, weaves, and hairstyles on manikins and from hair magazines in her hair salon named, *Perfection*. Brooke not only had fun with her cousin Jill, but she also loved being around her aunt Pam, observing her interaction and hair styling routines she gave each of her customers.

Brooke felt like she was in heaven, looking at so many varieties of hair textures and colors of hair from her aunt Pam's clients, whose hairstyles were straight, curly, and wavy of natural hair, wigs, and weaves.

As the weeks passed by, Brooke would go back to her Grandma Lu's house, and she would share the excitement of her days at the hair salon with her aunt Pam, and her cousin Jill at the hair salon. Brooke would also see her parents visit her occasionally, and she would tell them how much fun she spent at her aunt Pam's hair salon. Brooke still felt there was emotional tension between her and her mother Barb. This was because, Brooke was not with Barb at her hair salon, *That Look*, and Barb felt jealous of her daughter's time with her sister-in-law Pam. However, Brooke's father was happy for his daughter, and although he missed her at home, he knew this time Brooke had with his parents and his sister was good for Brooke and her future ambitions. He hoped she would pursue later as a career, to become a professional hairstylist like her mom, grandmother, and aunt.

So over the summer, Brooke continued to hang out with her aunt Pam weekly, on Saturdays. Brooke's dad would even stop by his sister Pam's hair salon to surprise her and the girls, Brooke and Jill on Saturdays, with bakery snacks. Brooke's father noticed how free-spirited his daughter was around his sister and cousin Jill, just like Brooke was around him, and he felt happy for his baby girl.

After a few weeks, late in the summer, on a Saturday, Pam, her daughter Jill, and Brooke were at Pam's hair salon working. Meanwhile, Pam was styling a client's hair with a curling iron, while the girls (Jill and Brooke) were sweeping the salon floor and fixing the hair magazines on the tables. Then surprisingly, Brooke's mom, Barb, showed up to be nosy, to visit and see what Brooke was up to. Not only was Brooke's mother trying to see what her competition was at her sister-in-law's hair shop, comparing it with her hair salon, but she was also trying to invite Brooke to her planned family event at the zoo for family day. Barb knew Brooke's dad couldn't make it because he had to work, but she wanted time alone with Brooke as mother and daughter to mend their relationship and have fun together. So Barb chatted with Pam for a minute, asking how she's been. Suddenly, Brooke heard her mother's voice in the hair salon while she and Jill were in the hair dryer room, and Brooke began to feel uncomfortable.

Jill looked over at Brooke and said happily, "There is Aunt Barb."

Brooke gave a half grin, feeling dread in her heart, and said, "Yes, I know."

Then Pam let's her client go, saying goodbye to her. Pam and Barb walked into the hair dryer room to greet the girls.

"Hi girls," said Barb to Brooke and Jill.

"Hi Mom," said Brooke with no emotion to her mother.

"Hi Aunt Barb," said Jill to Brooke's mother.

Pam said, "Brooke, your mom wants to steal you away to take you to a zoo trip today. Isn't that exciting?"

Brooke did not feel interested and tried to hide her unhappiness, and replied to her aunt Pam and mother, asking, "Is Dad going to be with us?"

"No baby, he had to work today, so it will be just us girls, mother-and-daughter time," said Brooke's mother.

Brooke hesitated for a few seconds, thinking she did not want to go without her dad and did not want to be alone with her mother, and then said, "I appreciate the invitation, but I don't feel like walking around the zoo today Mom, sorry." Barb and Pam looked at Brooke astonished, while Jill had a blank stare on her face.

Barb's anger was kindled in her heart against her daughter Brooke. She tried to hide her anger by gritting her teeth, and she looked at Brooke and kindly asked, "Why, baby? This would be a good time for you and I to catch up on our girl time."

Pam looked closely at her niece Brooke to see how she would respond.

"I rather go when Dad is able, that's all," Brooke replied.

"Well . . . I see," Barb responded with disappointment on her face and with her tone.

Pam felt bad for Barb because she sensed Brooke was not comfortable with her, but she did not want to interfere with Barb and Brooke's family issues. Pam looked over at Barb, shrugging, as if to say to Barb she was sorry Brooke didn't want to go. Barb felt like her heart had dropped and felt speechless.

Then Barb asked Brooke, "Will you go if we plan a day your father is not at work?"

Brooke nodded yes.

"Alrighty, I will talk to your father and reschedule. Well, love you, baby, let me get going," said Barb to her daughter Brooke.

Barb barely hugged her daughter Brooke and her niece Jill, just as one of Pam's other clients was walking in the hair salon.

Pam said to Brooke and Jill, "You girls can continue keeping the shop nice and tidy." (Brooke and Jill smiled and started chattering, as one of them started sweeping the shop floor and the other holding the dust pan). Pam then followed Barb to the salon's door, saying, "I'm glad you stopped by, and I am so sorry Brooke doesn't want to go."

Barb, feeling envy in her heart, gave Pam a fake smile and said, "It's not your fault. Brooke and I got some issues to work through. Thank you for being there for her."

"For sure. See you later Barb, and tell my brother Craig hello."

"Yes, I will," Barb replied, walking away to her gold Chevy truck. Barb pulled off in a hurry, as Pam closed her salon screen door and walked over to her new hair client, to look at a new weave her client brought in for her to sew on her head.

Pam pondered in her heart how sad Barb was feeling, and planned to talk to her mom Lucy about it later. When Pam was finished with her client, she sneaked away to another room in the salon, away from the girls, but where she could still see the girls in view, and called her mother Lucy to tell her about Barb's visit.

So the rest of the day went well for Pam and the girls.

Later, Brooke was dropped off to Grandma Lu's house by her aunt Pam. Aunt Pam waited for Brooke to walk in Lucy's house before she drove away. Pam and Jill waved at Brooke. Then Pam waved at her mother Lucy as her mother Lucy waved back at her and Jill. Then Pam drove away.

Grandma Lu was already informed about the visit of Brooke's mother and planned to talk to her granddaughter Brooke later about it.

First, Grandma Lu asked Brooke about her day, and Brooke was so happy as usual, sharing her day with her Grandma Lu. Then Grandma Lu told her to go wash her hands and change clothing to prepare for dinnertime soon. Grandma Lu told her to walk quietly because her grandfather was resting. Brooke obeyed her grandmother and walked through the kitchen to the bathroom to wash her hands and then to the guest room to change clothing.

Meanwhile, Grandma Lu was in the kitchen, cooking and thinking of a clever way to discuss with Brooke her feelings about her mother to try to encourage Brooke to forgive her mother for the previous wig conflict between them. Brooke returned into the kitchen to chat with her grandmother Lu while she was stirring the smothered potatoes in a frying pan. Grandma Lu handed Brooke a red apple, and a small glass of iced tea, and Brooke cheerfully sat in a chair to enjoy her apple and iced tea.

"So you had a good day?" Grandma Lu asked Brooke.

"Yes, Aunt Pam and Jill are so cool to be around, Grandma Lu," Brooke responded.

Grandma Lu smiled at her and said, "That's nice. I heard your mother stopped by Pam's shop today."

Brooke hesitantly looked at her grandmother with a countenance of irritation. Brooke said, "Yes, she did."

"She invited you to a zoo trip today and you said no?" Grandma Lu asked Brooke.

"Grandma Lu, I just didn't feel up to it today, especially without Dad," Brooke stated.

"I understand darling, but your mom wanted some time with you, maybe to make things right in your relationship together."

Brooke looked at her Grandma Lu with sincerity, respecting her grandmother's words.

"Yeah, but, Grandma Lu, after the incident with the wig before, my mom seems to not be sensitive to me as a young lady like Dad. I always feel restricted and not important to her. Dad doesn't make me feel that way. He respects how I feel and isn't so quick to punish me like Mom," Brooke explained.

Grandma Lu nodded, showing sympathy toward Brooke.

Grandma Lu then said, "When a mother sees her child growing up and wanting to look more mature, especially if she is into beauty and hair styling, some women panic when they see their little girl growing up. They think is too fast, and they overreact because they don't want to lose their little girl."

Brooke looked at her Grandma Lu with compassion, feeling remorse about her rejection of her mother that day.

Brooke asked, "Did you go through this with Aunt Pam when she was younger?"

Grandma Lu chuckled and smiled at Brooke, saying, "Yes. As a matter of fact, when I was a hairstylist, she started trying on my wigs at the age of five, and I had to stop her then with her little mature self. Then by the time she had gotten ten years old, I would catch her sneaking to try on my wigs at my hair salon when clients were not around. One day she begged me, could she wear one of my shorter wigs to the school pep rally for a sports event the school was having, and she liked this little boy she was trying to impress. She tried to convince me the day of the pep rally, could she wear it for that day, I said no, I would fix her hair pretty because she always had a long length of hair. But, it was not enough for your aunt Pam.

She liked the different colors of my wigs, but I did not let her wear them. So she wasn't happy with me at first. But once I styled her hair nice and pretty that day to look almost exactly like the wig she wanted to wear, she felt better, and that was the end of that. I know I inspired her later to become a beautician, and I am so proud of her."

Brooke adored her grandmother Lu, and was touched in her heart by the story she shared with her about her feelings regarding her aunt Pam growing up into womanhood as a mother, and how she tried to accommodate her aunt Pam with boundaries regarding how she wore her hair.

Brooke smiled and said, "Thank you Grandma Lu, for sharing that memory. It really helped me see things differently, from my mom's perspective." Brooke kissed her grandmother on her face cheek, and Grandma Lu also kissed her granddaughter face cheek, and they hugged.

Brooke then said, "Should I call Mom to try to reschedule with her?"

"No, just wait until she talks to your dad, until they plan a day to take you together, and from there, just try to be nicer to your mom, okay?"

Brooke looked at her grandmother Lu, smiling, and said, "Yes, okay."

Shortly after Grandma Lu's conversation with Brooke, Grandpa Dale walked into the kitchen, smiling at them, and asked, "Is dinner ready?"

Grandma Lu says, "Yes, let me get our plates."

That evening Brooke, as usual, enjoyed dinnertime with her grandparents, and she had a new perspective on how to start forgiving her mom. Brooke's grandmother influenced her perception of her mom, and Brooke had planned to try to let go of the bitterness she was feeling toward her mom in her heart. Although she felt this was a struggle internally for her, she hoped in time she could one day build a better relationship with her mom.

The following week, Brooke met with her parents to go on a trip with them to the zoo. Brooke was so happy to go because she was told by her grandmother Lu her dad would be going, and this was why she went. Brooke's parents picked her up in her father's burgundy truck, and she was so excited to hang out with her dad more than with her mother. As Craig was driving the truck to the zoo, he and Brooke had a good conversation. They talked about her summer with Grandma Lu, Aunt Pam, and Cousin Jill. Brooke had little words to say to her mother. They finally arrived at the zoo, and Brooke was excited to see the tigers and lions because they were her favorite animals. Barb adored the same animals as Brooke, and Barb tried to bond with her daughter by asking would she like Brooke to take a photo with her by the tigers. Brooke hesitated and looked at her dad. He smiled at her. Brooke then said to her mother, "Sure, why not?"

Barb smiled and gave her cell phone camera to Craig to get a good snapshot of them standing close together by the beautiful tigers. Craig took the photo as they both smiled. Barb felt hopeful, and she, Brooke, and Craig continued to walk around the zoo, looking at other animals, such as the bears.

An hour later, Craig asked Brooke, "Are you hungry baby?"

"Yes!" Brooke said anxiously.

Craig said, "Why don't we get a bite to eat at the food court?" Craig then asked Barb, "You okay with that, honey?"

Barb looked at him and said, "Sure, I am starving."

As all three of them walked into the zoo building lobby, Brooke was intrigued by the zoo gift shop they walked past. Barb noticed. Barb then suggested, "Brooke, darling, do you want to stop in the gift shop?"

Brooke said cheerfully, "Sure."

Craig smiled and followed Barb and Brooke in the gift shop.

Brooke looked at the animal figures and then walked over to hair accessories with animal prints. "Wow, these are pretty!" Brooke stated.

Barb looked over the headbands with Brooke and said, "They sure are." Barb began to think this may be the perfect opportunity to ask Brooke about how things were going at the hair shop with her and Aunt Pam, and her mother tried to propose her working at her hair shop with her, instead of at Aunt Pam's.

"Sooo... you enjoying yourself at Grandma Lu and Grandpa's house and Aunt Pam's shop?" Barb asked reluctantly.

Craig was watching with suspicion. Brooke looked at her mother with a blank stare and said, "Yes, I am having fun."

As they were walking around the gift shop, Barb then said, "I was thinking you can work at the shop with me some time. I think you can handle it now, and I can pay you more than your aunt Pam."

Craig looked disgruntled at Barb and looked at Brooke to study her response.

"Thanks Mom, but, I am cool with Aunt Pam," said Brooke, and Brooke walked away distracted, looking at jewelry on the other side of the gift shop.

As Brooke was walking around the gift shop, away from her parents, Craig whispered to Barb, "Really Barb, why would you bring that up right now?"

Barb, shaking her head in dismay, whispered to Craig, "Why not? I am only trying to bond with my daughter."

Craig replied in a whisper, looking at Brooke away from them, "This is not the time Barb."

Craig then noticed Brooke walking toward them, and she had a pair of tiger earrings in her hands, and she asked her dad, "Can you buy these for me?"

Craig put his arms around Brooke's shoulders and said, "Sure, anything pretty for my princess."

Brooke smiled, as they walked up to the register to pay for the earrings. Barb was silent and feeling rejected and troubled about her daughter.

From the gift shop, they walked to the cafeteria and ordered a meal of burgers, fries, and soft drinks, and had lunch together.

Although Brooke conversed with both of her parents about the zoo trip, admiring the animals they saw, she talked more with her dad than her mom. Craig noticed this, and Barb continued to feel indifferent about the trip. After lunch, they continued to walk around the zoo to visit the elephants, and a half hour later, they left the zoo, and Brooke's parents took her back to the house of Craig's parents.

Brooke was happy about the time she had at the zoo, especially because she got to be with her dad. Both of her parents said goodbye to her for the evening, as they pulled off in Craig's truck. Brooke bragged to her grandparents about how much fun she had at the zoo, and the earrings she received.

Meanwhile, driving home, Craig and Barb were having a hard discussion in Craig's truck, about their future parenting of their daughter Brooke, and Barb's troubled feelings about Brooke not wanting to spend time with her at her own hair salon. Craig continued to be optimistic, and encouraged Barb to take it one day at a time, and to continue to parent Brooke the best way they could, with parental love and sensitivity. He asked Barb to stop meddling with other family relationships, that Brooke chose to have with good people in his family, and allow their daughter to make her own decisions about family, as long as she was safe.

Chapter 3

The Battle of the Hair

A month later, in August, Aunt Pam had a conversation with Brooke about her hair. Brooke expressed to her in words she hated her relaxed perm hair, that it was too short, and she was interested in trying to change to her natural curly hair, to see how much volume and longer it could grow. Pam pondered in her thoughts, how she would approach her sister-in-law, Barb, about the hair change of her daughter, Brooke, without offending her. So later that week, Aunt Pam called Barb to ask her if she could help Brooke transition to natural hair. Barb felt emotionally furious, and became emotionally jealous of Pam getting involved with the development of her daughter's appearance. Barb suppressed her emotions and said politely on the phone to Pam, she would get back to her about Brooke's hair transition, while she was in Pam's care. Barb wanted to talk to Craig, her husband about it first.

When Craig arrived home that evening, Barb was watching television, but looking disturbed.

Craig noticed and said, "Hey, you okay? How was your day?"

Barb looked at her husband Craig and responded with a gloomy attitude, "As usual, another hard day for your good ole wife."

Craig looked at her confused and asked, "So what is that supposed to mean?"

Barb replied with haste, "Your daughter had the nerve to ask your sister, if she can change her *relaxed hair to natural hair*, and she wants your sister to help her instead of me."

Craig widened his eyes for a moment and shrugged carelessly, as if Barb, his wife, was overreacting, and he said hesitantly, "Sooo what is wrong with that Barb?"

"Really Craig? That's our daughter, not your sister's. I knew I did not want her to go live over your parent's house, because now, Brooke thinks she is too grown, and is making decisions without us!" shouted Barb.

Craig responded in a huff and puff, saying, "It is not about my sister. It is your insecurity and jealousy of her, that she can influence our daughter, and make her happy in ways you can't Barb! With our work schedules and the way you treated Brooke about your precious wig, our daughter made her own decision on how she feels about you. So do not blame my sister, her aunt Pam, for this."

Barb looked sorrowful. In her heart, she knew her husband was right. Before the summer, her treatment of their daughter was heartless and insensitive, and she was trying to find ways to restore a good relationship with her daughter, but she seemed to struggle with how.

Barb then said to her husband Craig, "I need to talk to my baby about this."

Craig looked at Barb with an unsettling stare, as he picked up the television remote to find a sports channel and said, "Be careful with your tone with Brooke, she's our daughter, and my sister Pam is just as a good beautician as you. Let Brooke decide, since she is not in our custody for the summer."

Meanwhile, at Pam's hair salon, she just finished with her last client for the day, and the girls (Jill and Brooke) were restless and cheerful, as they were helping sweep customers' hair left on the salon floor.

"All right girls, as soon as you finish up sweeping, would you girls like a burger and some fries, for doing such a good job today, before I take Brooke to Grandma Lu's?"

"Yes!" the girls shouted happily.

As Pam was putting away her hair tools, Jill noticed her mom reach into one of her high cabinets to grab some natural hair Mielle products that were new, and never opened, to put in separate bag to take with her. Jill was puzzled about this because, Jill hair was already natural, shoulder-length, and her mom never took Mielle salon products home.

So Jill asked her mom, "Mom, who are the Mielle products for?

Do we need some at home?"

Pam looked startled at her daughter Jill and then her niece Brooke, and she hesitantly said, "Well . . . this maybe for Brooke."

Brooke looked surprised and felt excitement and said, "For me Aunt Pam?"

Pam said, "Well, that is . . . if your mom gives me permission. She wanted first to talk it over with your dad, and she will let me know soon."

Brooke gave a half grin and said, "I so hope she says yes. I know Dad will, but Mother is another story."

Barb called Pam a day later and asked could she speak with Brooke by phone. When Brooke spoke to her mother by phone, Barb asked Brooke would she consider her helping transition her hair instead of her aunt Pam. When Brooke said she would rather Aunt Pam care for her hair, Barb felt so upset within her heart, but hid her emotions over the phone.

So Barb said firmly to Brooke, "I'm sorry, then you need to wait until you get older before you change your perm hair to natural hair, to no longer use perm chemicals in your hair, and we will talk about it again soon."

"Why?" Brooke asked with disgust. Meanwhile, Pam was observing the phone conversation, shaking her head with disappointment for Brooke.

Barb said, "Because you are not old enough yet to make decisions about your hair, and I am your mother, I would rather take care of you hair. Don't I have the right Brooke?"

Brooke was silent, holding the phone for a few seconds, and she said, "Mom, I have to go, thanks anyway. I will give Aunt Pam the phone."

Barb felt horrible, but wanted to keep control over Brooke's life, and tears filled her eyes, as Pam started talking on the phone to her.

"Hello Barb," said Pam, sounding concerned.

"Hi Pam, I'm sorry, you probably already know. I want Brooke to wait until she gets a little older, and since she doesn't want me, as her mother, to care for her hair, I decided she should wait."

Pam's face looked disappointed. She put the call on speaker phone, but she respected Barb as a mother and said, "Okay, Barb, I understand. She's your daughter, it's your decision. I just thought I could help do something nice for Brooke as my niece."

Barb face looking frustrated, responded with a firm tone, "I appreciate your concern Pam, but she must have some boundaries, and when she is a teen, she can make more decisions about her hair then." Brooke and Jill heard Barb's words, and they looked at each other and shrugged, trying to accept Barb's decision.

51

"Okay Barb, well, let me go. I need to finish closing my shop. We will talk again soon," Pam stated.

"All right Pam, have a good day," Barb said.

"You too Barb." The phone call ended.

"Oh my goodness, Aunt Pam, my mother is so unfair!" Brooke said with anger.

Pam tried to comfort her by saying, "I'm so sorry, Brooke, I know this is frustrating to you, but she is your mother, and we have to respect her wishes. Look on the bright side, she did say when you become a teen, you can make more decisions about your hair."

Brooke said sarcastically, "By that time, I may be bald by then."

Jill laughed, and Pam smiled and said, "Don't talk like that, you got plenty of time for hair care. In the meantime, you girls finish straightening the shop so we can go get some burgers and fries."

The girls smiled and continued to move around cleaning the shop and folding hair towels in another room.

Pam made sure the coast was clear, and she decided to quick call her brother Craig, Brooke's father, to tell him about his conversation with his wife, and get his take on Barb's decision.

Craig answered the phone with joy. "Hey sis, how's it going with you and the two trouble makers, Brooke and Jill?"

Pam laughed and said, "I am fine, and the two angel girls are fine. How you been?"

"Well, life is good, and I thank you for blessing my baby girl, but Barb has been impossible, complaining about the time Brooke spends with you instead of her," Craig said.

"Well, yeah, speaking of your wife, I just spoke on the phone with her concerning caring for Brooke's hair, to stop putting perm in her hair and me asking to help Brooke go natural because, that is what Brooke wants, and Barb, God love her, just shut the whole idea down, talking about Brooke is too young to make that decision and so on. And when Brooke tried to talk to her, it didn't go so well. I just feel like Barb is jealous and feels competitive about our hair salons, and me caring for your daughter's hair."

Craig said sympathetically, "Pam, you are absolutely right. I love my wife, but her and Brooke's relationship has never been quite the same since that wig incident last school semester. Brooke seems happier with Mom and Dad, because I work late during the week, she hardly spends much time with me, and her time alone with her mother is tension and a challenge. However, I will keep trying to encourage Brooke to respect her mother, but to also be in tuned with her own identity, and to be able to express her feelings in conversation and choices in a healthy way."

"You're such a good father to her Craig," said Pam.

"Thanks sis, and you are a good mother to Jill, and also a good aunt to my baby girl. We must try to have lunch soon just for old time's sake."

"Yes Craig, we must soon, just you and I, brother and sister lunch at a chicken restaurant."

Craig chuckled and said, "I will keep you posted on my schedule."

"Sounds good. Well, I am about to take the girls to a burger place now. They have worked so hard in my shop. Then I will be taking Brooke to Mom and Dad's, until you pick her up on Sunday to visit you and Barb at your home."

"Okay, tell my baby I love her, and I will talk to you later. Love you and Jill," Craig replied.

"Love you too Craig," Pam responded. Their phone call ended well.

Pam took the girls, as promised, to the burger place, and they enjoyed burgers, fries, and cola drinks in the restaurant, laughing and having fun.

As the summer was near the end, and weeks passed, Brooke resented her mom even more, and their relationship remained distant and awkward. Finally, summer ended, and although Brooke enjoyed her summer with her grandparents and Aunt Pam and Cousin Jill, she was somewhat sad to have to return home for the school season. However, Brooke was still able to work at her aunt Pam's hair salon on weekends, when her dad dropped her off there, and regularly visit her grandparents on some weekends and holidays, and eventually, stay with her grandparents every summer.

Chapter 4

The Mysterious Wonder Wig

Brooke had finally become a teenager, sixteen years of age. On the weekends, she continued to have mainly her dad's support to continue to work at her aunt Pam's hair salon. One day, Brooke saw this fascinating, beautiful wig that was shoulder-length wavy blond-brown. It caught Brooke's eye. Brooke, being a teen, was more conscious of her looks than ever. So Brooke asked her aunt Pam if she could look at the manikins' heads with the new wigs. As Brooke walked over to the wig she adored, her aunt Pam noticed her try the wig on, and Pam smiled.

Jill said, "It looks gorgeous on you Brooke!"

Brooke looked at herself, admiring how she looks in the hair salon mirror, as lady customers were commenting how cute she looked.

Then Brooke sneaked away to the hair supply room in the salon, to play with the wig on her head by herself. Then surprisingly, a weird thing happened, when Brooke tried on the wavy blond-brown wig, the wig glowed beautifully on her own head. Brooke was shocked, and almost breathless. Then within seconds, there was another dramatic thing she discovered, that was even more odd for her, as she wore the special wig, like a radio, she could hear conversations of students with alopecia from her school and medical clinics. *Wow!* Brooke thought to herself, and she trembled. This unusual wig completely startled her because, it had special powers, but she was too much in shock, to tell her aunt Pam and her cousin Jill.

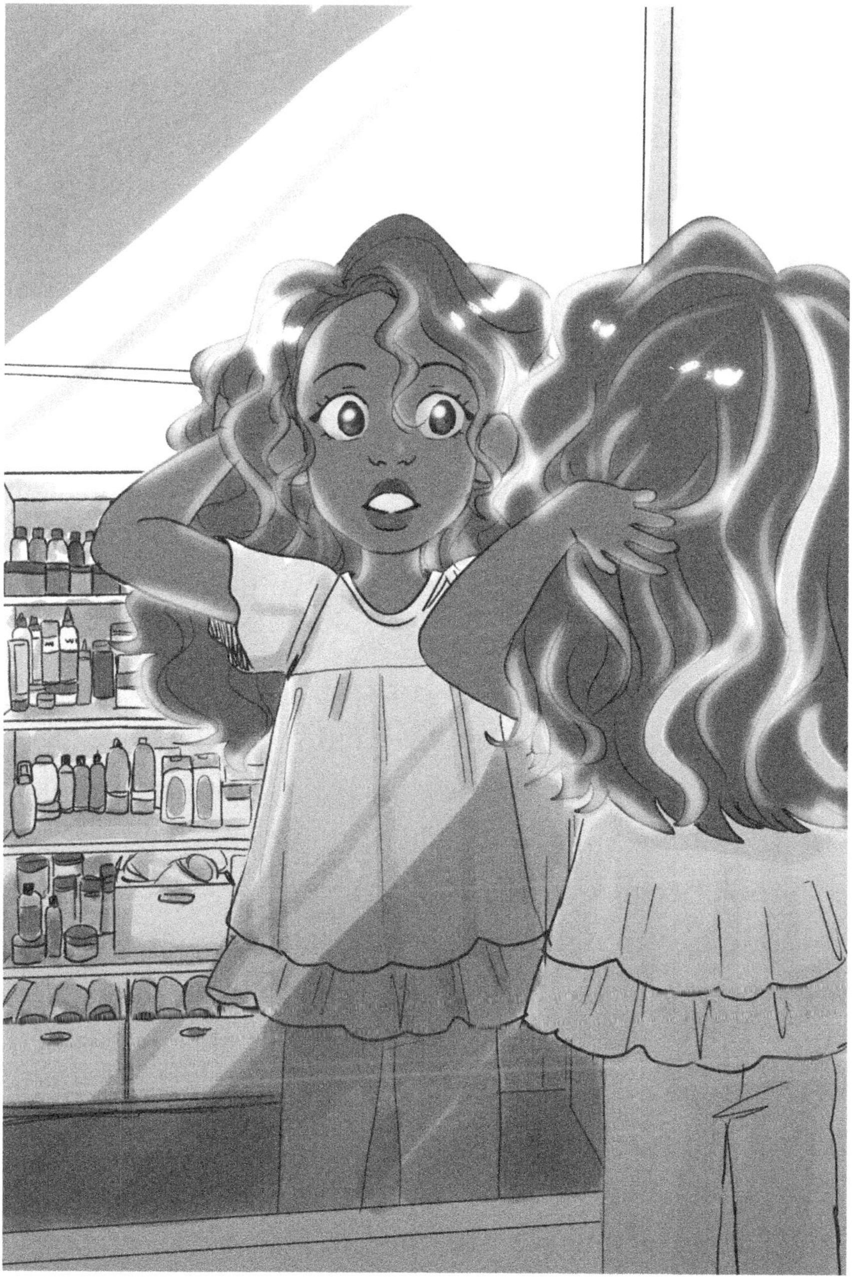

At the same time, she admired the power of this peculiar wig, as it also made her feel super confident and beautiful, right before her very eyes. Then suddenly, she heard Jill calling for her. "Brooke, where are you with Mom's wig?" Brooke heard Jill chuckling. Brooke quickly removed the wig to avoid anyone from hearing what she could hear from the special wig. Then Jill found Brooke looking in a mirror in the hair supply room, meddling with the wavy wig. Jill quickly snatched the wig from Brooke's hands, as a joke. Brooke, frightened, said loudly, "No Jill!"

Brooke thought that Jill would hear what she heard from the wig, but what was strange, Jill could not hear anything from the special wig.

Jill asked in an offensive way, "What's wrong with you? I was only playing with you."

Brooke responded, "I'm sorry, Jill, I just didn't like you snatching the wig from me like that."

Jill handed Brooke the wig and said, I'm sorry Brooke, but Mom is looking for you."

Brooke replied, "I will be right there," as thoughts were racing through her mind about what just happened with the wig, and she wondered where were the people and the hair events taking place, that she discovered hearing about, from wearing this mesmerizing wig. After Jill walked away, Brooke began staring at her new radiant wig with amazement.

So Brooke quickly put the wig back on her head, and she felt more confident, and again she could hear conversations of people talking about hair events, and alopecia. The wig was revealing secret information about mysterious people, who needed special hair care.

Afterwards, Brooke, with hesitation, slowly pulled and removed the wig from her head. Brooke's eyes widened with amazement, as she thoroughly looked inside and outside the new top secret wig.

She said to herself, "I can't tell anyone about this... I will call this my *wonder wig*." Brooke quickly put the wig back on, hoping she could hear more conversations about hair, and she did, but the voices quickly faded. Brooke carefully took the wig off her head again. With the wig in her hand, trying to act normal, Brooke smiled and walked suspiciously in the main salon room, where Aunt Pam and Jill were watching television. Aunt Pam looked at Brooke and smiled and said, "Sneaking off with my wig?"

Brooke smiled and said, "I am sorry Aunt Pam, I couldn't resist. It is so beautiful. Can I keep it?"

Aunt Pam said to Brooke, "You know what, if you clean my salon bathroom and wash all the hair towels, you can have it today."

Brooke's eyes widened, and her smile was so huge, and she put the wig in a corner cabinet to be tucked away for safekeeping and got right to the chores her aunt Pam requested, and Jill followed Brooke in the salon laundry room to help. After Brooke and Jill were done with their cleaning chores of the hair salon, Brooke sneaked over to the cabinet where she put her special *wonder wig*, glancing at the wig, admiring the soft strands of hair on the glamorous wig. A few minutes later, Aunt Pam said,

"Brooke, take your wig with you," before she noticed Brooke taking it out of the cabinet where Brooke hid the wig. Brooke smiled and looked at her aunt Pam and Jill.

Jill said, "Mom, she already has it."

Aunt Pam looked over at Brooke as she got her purse and keys and said, "You sneaky thing! Come on, little smarty, let's go get some pizza."

Laughing, Aunt Pam, Brooke, and Jill walked out of the hair salon. Pam locked her hair shop's doors. The girls had a good time having lunch with Pam.

Later, Aunt Pam took Brooke to Grandma Lu's. Brooke showed Grandma Lu the wig with excitement. Grandma Lu checked out the wig, held it in her hands, and tried to put it on herself.

Brooke delicately and quickly grabbed the wig from her grandmother and said, "Sorry, Grandma Lu, I still need to style my new wig, don't want you to try it on until I comb it a little."

Grandma Lu, looking puzzled and amused at her granddaughter Brooke, said, "Okay, so protective of this show-stopping wig, if you say so."

Brooke smiled and hugged her grandmother. Then she walked toward her grandmother's guest room that was set aside for her, as Grandma Lu watched Brooke closely, walk to her room, and she smiled, happy for her granddaughter. When Brooke noticed her grandmother wasn't looking at her anymore, Brooke slowly closed her guest room door, and she hid her *wonder wig*, in one of her dresser cabinets.

Later that evening, Brooke shared with her grandparents stories about her day at Aunt Pam's salon, over a delicious chicken meal, and as usual, they enjoyed their granddaughter's company for the day.

The following day, Brooke didn't take the wig home, nor did she tell her grandparents the super powers of the wig. Brooke knew the special wig was safe at Grandma Lu's house. Then later, Grandma Lu decided to call her son Craig, and they both had small talk together by phone. Then Grandma Lu mentioned to him, that his daughter earned a dazzling new wig, from his sister Pam, and Grandma was wondering if Brooke took it home with her. Grandma Lu didn't know, Brooke intentionally left the wig at her house. So Craig told his mom he would ask his daughter Brooke, did she leave her new wig at his mother's house? After Craig's phone call with his mother, he began to ponder, if Brooke left her new wig at his mother's house on purpose, to avoid conflict with his wife Barb later. So Craig kept the matter to himself and decided he would address Brooke privately about the wig later.

Then a few days later, at Brooke's school, there was a hair and fashion-modeling contest announced to raise money for college tuition for future graduates at her school, and Brooke wanted to win this contest badly. Brooke felt she had a chance with her new wig, but she hadn't told her parents, and she needed to get their permission to enter the beauty contest. So she planned to muster up the courage to ask her parents later.

CHAPTER 5

Brooke's Awareness to Alopecia

Meanwhile, Brooke began to notice a couple of girls with alopecia in school, and she remembered when she privately put on her *wonder wig,* she could hear some of these girls conversations about their hair troubles, talking with their families or friends, and Brooke emotionally felt a sense of grief about the condition of their hair. Brooke was very sympathetic toward them, not because she ever had this hair disease, but because she always struggled with her own personal feelings about her hair she often wore in a weaved hair bun, and she never felt confident about how it looked. So this made Brooke eager, to help these girls, and she thought of a plan to ask her aunt Pam, how she could give some of the girls at her school free wigs, as a gift, to help boost their confidence.

Although Brooke wanted to win the modeling contest, she still wanted to help the two girls in her school with the hair scalp disease.

She also knew her *wonder wig,* gave her an advantage, how to look better, and she planned to use the *wonder wig* in the beauty contest. However, Brooke knew she could also help the girls at her school resolve any hair problems, offering good wigs, Although Brooke did not want to reveal her secret about her *wonder wig,* and the powers it had, she was determined to help these girls needing a hair makeover.

So one day, when Brooke was working on a Saturday for her aunt Pam, and with her cousin Jill, Brooke asked her aunt Pam, if she could do more cleaning chores, in her aunt Pam's hair shop, to earn more pay, to buy two silky wavy black wigs, she saw her aunt Pam keep in her beauty supply bags, in one of her salon cabinets.

Her Aunt Pam asked with curiosity, "Brooke, now what are you going to do with two of the same wigs?"

Brooke smiled and said, "Aunt Pam, I want to buy these as a gift for two girls at my school who struggle with alopecia." Jill stopped watching the hair salon television, and began listening with interest, to Brooke's conversation with her mom because, she had never heard Brooke speak about this before.

Aunt Pam smiled with amazement and said, "I think that is admirable, you want to help girls at your school with their appearance and self-confidence, but alopecia? How do you know about alopecia, and why are you so interested in helping them?"

Brooke responded, "I just know from hearing about it, and I can understand how a girl feels when she doesn't like her hair."

Aunt Pam looked into Brooke's eyes, and could see how serious Brooke was about this matter. Just as a hair client was walking in the hair salon, Aunt Pam paused, and looked at Brooke with admiration, and said, "Sure, you can buy the two black wavy wigs from me later today, but first, can you stock those sodas in the vending machine, and then put a load of the hair shop towels in the washing machine in the laundry room?"

Brooke smiled and said cheerfully, "Gladly, thanks Aunt Pam."

Jill looked at Brooke walking toward the sodas, and was puzzled about her effort to earn wigs, but Jill adored her cousin Brooke and said to Brooke, "That's cool, cousin, let me know if you need any help."

Brooke grinned at Jill and said, "Thank you, I will."

Jill then walked toward the hair salon lobby, got a broom, and began sweeping the salon floor for her mother, Pam.

Later that evening, when the hair shop was about to close, Aunt Pam took a deep breath, and thanked the girls for their help that day. Then she paid each of them $35 for the day, and gave Brooke the bag of two brand new shoulder-length brunette wigs.

Brooke was so excited and said, "Thanks Aunt Pam," and she hugged her aunt.

Aunt Pam said, "You are welcome, you earned it. I see your father parking his truck outside. See you later sweetie."

"Okay, bye Aunt Pam, bye Jill," Brooke said happily, as she left the hair shop, and walked to her father's truck. Pam waved at her brother Craig from the hair shop window door. Craig waved back at his sister Pam and niece Jill, and then Craig drove away with Brooke.

"How was your day, young lady?" Craig asked his daughter Brooke.

Brooke responded with excitement, "Dad, my day was great, and look what I earned from Aunt Pam, two beautiful wavy brunette wigs, I want to give these girls at school who have alopecia."

Brooke's dad smiled in shock, and he asked with curiosity, "Alopecia? How did you learn of this? Did they talk to you about it?"

Brooke was hesitant about answering her dad because, she didn't want to tell him about her *wonder wig*. He didn't know it had special powers to reveal information to her about people with hair problems. But, Brooke did not know, Grandma Lu already told her dad, Brooke brought another new wig to her grandmother's house.

So Brooke smirked and said, "Um, I overheard one of their conversations in the girls' bathroom by the sink at school, and they seemed insecure about their short hair in the bathroom school mirror."

Brooke's dad responded, "Oh okay. Well, that is a very commendable thing that you are trying to do for these young ladies, and your Mom will be proud of you too." Her dad continued to say, "Brooke, don't you have another wig? Your Grandma Lu called me earlier, and told me, you brought a different new wig to her house?"

Brooke looked dumbstruck and hesitantly said, "Oh yeah, I do have a wig Aunt Pam gave me for myself, but I didn't want to bring it home just yet." Brooke's countenance changed to a blank expression.

Craig glanced at his daughter, and then back on the road, as he was driving them home in his truck and said, "Are you worried about what your mother is going to say?"

"Dad, yes, and although I am old enough to make my own decisions about my hair, I don't want the criticism or judgment, so when I am ready to wear it, I will tell her then," Brooke replied.

"Okay young lady, I won't say a word. You are a responsible teen and young lady, and I trust your judgment. You tell her when you ready, no big deal," Brooke's father said with a smile.

Brooke felt content and smiled at her dad with joy in her heart and said, "Thanks Daddy, love you."

Craig looked at his daughter and said, "Love you too baby."

Brooke and her dad finally arrive home, and Barb, smiling, met them in the driveway. Barb noticed Brooke holding a bag. She could tell those were wigs. Barb said hello to her husband and Brooke, and looked strangely at

Brooke's bag. Brooke noticed her mom staring at her bag, as they all walked through their house door.

Barb touched Brooke's hair bag and said, "Hey, what is this I see, wigs? How did you get these—Aunt Pam?"

Brooke felt grieved in her heart but, trying to be respectful to her Mom, "Oh, these two wigs I earned from Aunt Pam, from cleaning chores at her hair salon this week."

Craig, looking concerned at his wife and daughter, remained quiet, observing their conversation.

Brooke's mom asked, "Can I see them?"

"Sure, Brooke replied, as she pulled the beautiful medium-length wigs from her salon bag.

Barb looked thoroughly at the two wigs, admiring their texture and sheen.

"Those are gorgeous, Brooke, but why do you have two of the same wigs?" her mother inquired.

Brooke said, "I want to give them as gifts to girls at my school that I noticed struggle with alopecia, to help them feel better about themselves."

Craig smiled at his daughter, as he sat down in his recliner, to read a sports magazine.

Barb was astonished, and felt emotions of guilt, as she put her hand over her mouth, thinking about how proud she was of her daughter's interest to help two girls with their hair, and she reflected on their wig spat years past, when Brooke used her wig for appearance and self-esteem issues.

Barb then handed the wigs over back to her daughter and said, "That is thoughtful of you, I am so proud of you, and you didn't even get a wig for yourself."

Brooke, thinking about her *wonder wig* at Grandma Lu's, not comfortable telling her mom, reluctantly said, "There is a modeling contest at school that Jill and I want to enter, but I need you and dad's signatures to enter the modeling contest that will be in three months. So the parents and the community will purchase tickets to attend the contest. The proceeds will raise money to prepare teens to get scholarships for college, when they graduate from high school. Also, I believe the winner receives a 5,000 reward towards his or her college tuition. Can I be in the contest?"

Although Brooke's dad was totally supportive of Brooke being in the beauty contest, Brooke's dad looked at Barb to try to make the decision with her. Brooke looked anxiously at both of her parents, waiting for their response together.

Barb looked at Brooke's eyes and saw the importance of the contest to her, and she surprisingly said, "Absolutely!"

Shocked but smiling, Brooke looked at her mom, and then she glanced at her dad, and then Brooke asked, "You mean it?"

Barb said, "Yes, you can win. You are beautiful enough, mature, and thoughtful of others, and it is for a good cause. Yes baby, I support you!"

In tears, Brooke rushed over to her mom and gave her a tight hug. Barb looked at her husband Craig smiling, and tears filled her eyes, as she embraced her daughter with love, and finally felt the emotional bond she missed with her daughter for a long time.

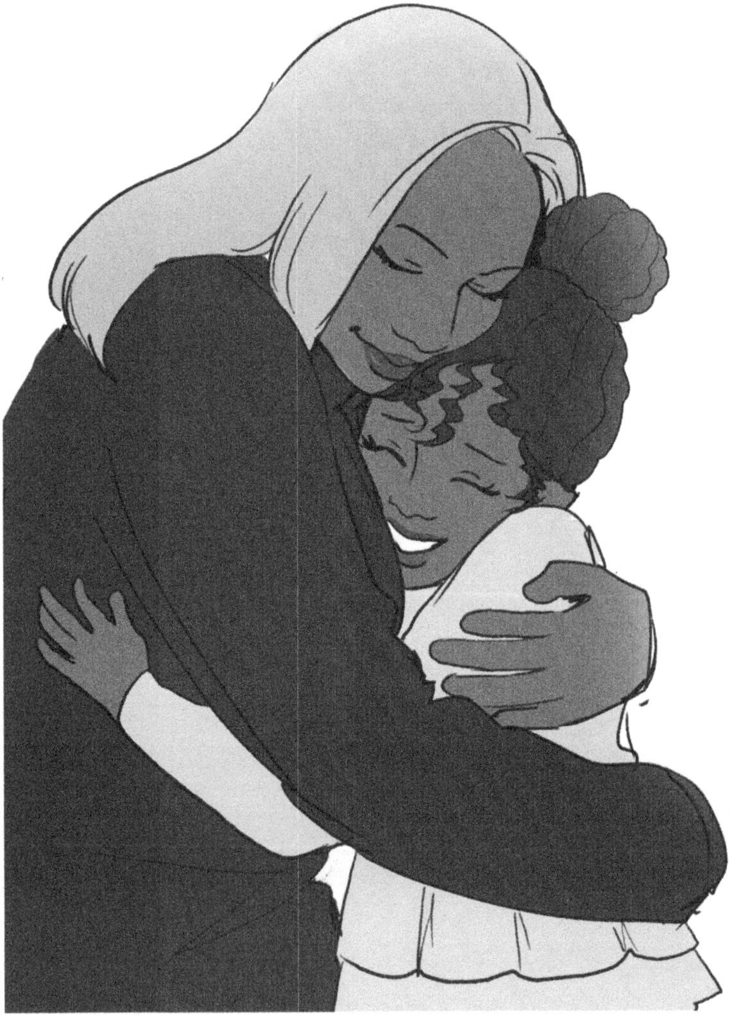

Brooke said with humility and gratitude to her mom, "This means so much to me. Thank you Mom."

Brooke's father said, "Yes, I am in agreement with your mom, you can win, and no matter what happens, we are proud of you."

Brooke ran over to her dad, and also hugged him tightly. Then she wiped her tears and said, "Thanks Daddy."

Chapter 6

"Wiggin It"- The Beauty Contest

For the next few months, before the beauty contest, Brooke decided to begin transitioning her hair from *relaxed perm hair to natural*. Although she didn't need her parents' permission for this process, and they were both aware, along with her aunt Pam's support, Brooke still struggled with the length of her hair and how to style it.

So one day, Brooke decided to wear a newer shoulder-length wavy reddish-color wig, she bought from her aunt Pam, which looked similar to her *wonder wig*. Brooke wanted to hide the coily thick shortness of her Afro hair, to enhance her look, similar to the look of her *wonder wig*. The reddish wig made her look and feel gorgeous with it on. Her aunt Pam never questioned how Brooke changed wigs. As a hairstylist, Aunt Pam would change wigs just as much as her niece, and this was an admirable thing for both of them. Brooke would only put on her *wonder wig* in private, at her Grandma Lu's house. During her own personal pampering time, Brooke would experiment with different looks, and hairstyles by herself, to admire the variety of looks, she imagined herself wearing. Finally, Brooke decided to take her *wonder wig* home, but hid it. She wanted to keep privately trying it on, and styling her *wonder wig*, until the day of the beauty contest, where Brooke planned to wear her *wonder wig* in public, to feel glamorous, and to surprise her parents, with the hope of winning the modeling contest.

The day of the beauty contest, Brooke was dressed in a sparkling gorgeous, dark purple gown, and a stylish dark purple hat, to temporarily cover her natural Afro hair. She did not realize, she grabbed the wrong bag of hair from one of her hair bags, which was a weave, instead of her *wonder wig*, when she was at her parent's house in preparation for the beauty contest. So by mistake, Brooke brought the wrong hair, in a bag to school, when her parents brought her to school, to continue preparing for the contest, in the girls' bathroom, with other contestants. Brooke was so happy to see one of the girls named Ruth. Ruth was one of the girls, Brooke secretly knew had alopecia; and Brooke had learned about Ruth's hair condition from her *wonder wig*. Brooke was so happy, when she noticed Ruth was wearing one of the wigs, Brooke gave Ruth as a gift, and Brooke admired Ruth's beautiful yellow dress. When Ruth saw Brooke, she happily held a short conversation with her, talking about the excitement of the contest. They both were left alone in the bathroom by the mirror sink, putting on a little make-up, and straightening their clothing, as other girls were leaving.

"Thank you so much Brooke, for giving me this wig. It has been life-changing to how I feel about myself altogether, my self-worth," said Ruth to Brooke.

Brooke smiled with tears and said, "Ruth, I felt honored to help you look pretty, and I hope one of us wins this contest."

Ruth said, "Yes, I agree, and the winner I heard gets, a $5000 scholarship toward their college tuition."

Brooke replied cheerfully, "Yes, I heard the same thing from my teacher few weeks ago. That would be such a blessing."

Then Ruth noticed Brooke with a bag of hair and asked, "Is that another wig?"

Brooke said eagerly, "Yes, I'm going to wear this new wig as a surprise for the contest."

Ruth said, "Wow, I can't wait to see. You have really been wiggin it, to be able to change to different hairstyles. Must be great to do that."

Brooke responded, "Yes, having a mom and an aunt who are beauticians really helps me."

Ruth replied, "Well, let me get in line backstage. See you soon."

Brooke hugged Ruth and said, "Yes, let me finish getting myself together quickly."

Ruth left Brooke in the bathroom by herself. Brooke looked at the bathroom door, hesitantly making sure no one was around, and she hurriedly grabbed her bundle of hair from her hair bag, just to be in complete shock, realizing that she had the wrong hair. "Oh no!" Brooke said to herself frantically. Brooke heart felt like it dropped, as she looked to see, she had a bag of weave hair, that was the same color as her *wonder wig*, but it was not her *wonder wig*. Brooke said to herself, "I grabbed the wrong hair, and there is no time to get the right one." Brooke immediately began to weep, grabbing paper towels to wipe her face, as she tried to decide if she would walk the stage. She didn't feel confident enough to wear her own hair, which was at that time, in a curly Afro style. She could hear the crowds outside the bathroom, walking toward the auditorium to prepare to see the show. She knew there were fifteen contestants, and she was number 2 to walk on the stage. Feeling a rush of anxiety, Brooke was thinking, she had to do something quickly, or back out of the contest.

Brooke suddenly heard her dad outside the bathroom door, saying, "Brooke, you all right? Your Mom and I are waiting for you. The show is about to start."

Brooke, sniffling and drying her eyes, said, "Daddy, I am fine, I will be right there."

"Okay sweetie, we are so proud of you," her dad replied as she heard his footsteps walk away.

Brooke thought to herself, she did not want to let down herself, or disappoint her parents, her Aunt Pam, her grandparents, or her friend Ruth. So Brooke decided with courage, she would remove her dark purple hat, and wear her own natural Afro hairstyle for the contest. So she looked in her purse, and used her hair comb to style it, and add some Mielle rice therapy hair lotion, she carried in her purse, to bring definition to her natural curls, and she finger coiled most of her hair quickly. She then hurriedly added more face powder and lipstick to her face. Then she looked at herself in the mirror and said, "Brooke, you can do this. There is no turning back now."

Brooke finally met the other contestants on stage, as she met up with Jill and Ruth, and they both smiled at Brooke in shock, noticing, she was not wearing a wig.

Jill asked, "Where is your wig?"

Brooke responded, "It's a long story, I will tell you later."

Ruth said to Brooke, "You changed your mind about the wig?"

Brooke smiled, trying to suppress the pain and fear in her heart, and said, "Yes, I decided to just be me."

Ruth admired Brooke's words and said, "You are my shero."

Brooke smiled as she looked into the audience, and she could see her parents, grandparents, Aunt Pam, and other classmates and teachers. Brooke felt nervous, but was ready to walk the stage and model.

The beauty contest finally began. Jill was the first one to be called, as she walked across the stage gracefully in a rose-colored dress. There were many hand claps, as Jill smiled and walked across the stage.

Next, it was Brooke's turn. She knew her parents and her family expected her to wear a wig, and Brooke was wondering what would they think when they see her walk across with a totally different look of her natural short hair. Brooke smiled, as she sashayed across the stage smiling, and feeling her heart beating like a drum, she looked into the audience at her parents, grandparents, her aunt Pam, and others in the audience. Her family immediately looked at Brooke, smiling with amazement, as many hand claps were heard, and lingered, while she walked the stage courageously. As Brooke met Jill backstage, Jill said, "You looked great, you did good."

Brooke was happy with the support she heard, but she felt sweaty and relieved it was over, and said to Jill, "Oh my goodness, people liked me, and you looked beautiful yourself."

Jill said, "Thank you cousin."

Just as other contestants were called, some with fewer hand claps from the audience than others, finally, Ruth was called.

Ruth suddenly snatched off her wig, then she put her hands through her hair, to quickly style it, as some bald areas showed around her head of hair. Ruth then walked across the stage with confidence, trying to follow suit to Brooke's bravery of no wig with her short hair.

Brooke looked at Ruth with admiration, and Brooke felt a great emotion of amazement, for the stance, Ruth took, walking across the stage with her wig in her hand, with humor, showing the audience the wig, as she walked across the stage.

For ten seconds, the auditorium was quiet, and suddenly, the hand claps were so loud, the noise sounded like a crowd at a sports game. Jill and Brooke looked at each other with joy about Ruth.

Brooke said to Jill, "She took off her wig with such boldness—wow, she is so special and courageous."

Jill smiled and said, "Just like you."

Afterwards, when Ruth walked backstage nervously, while the other contestants were being called to walk the stage, Pam with excitement appeared, to talk to the girls. At the same time, Brooke hugged Ruth and said, "You are amazing! What made you take off your wig?"

Ruth said, "You—you, Brooke, inspired me to, and I feel just as beautiful and free, with no wig, just as I do with the wig."

Pam hugged her daughter Jill and said, "You did great." Then she looked at Brooke and said, "Niece, I am so proud of you. What happen to your wig?"

Brooke grinned and said, "Aunt Pam, I left my wig at home. I didn't know I didn't have it until the last minute. I accidentally brought my bag of weave, instead of my wig, and I had no choice but to wear my hair."

Jill laughed and said to Brooke, "So that's what happened?"

Brooke looked at her, Aunt Pam, and Ruth and said, "Yes."

"Your mom and dad and Grandma Lu and Grandpa Dale asked me to check on you girls, and they told me to tell you, they are proud of you both, and you too, Ruth."

All three girls smiled.

Then Aunt Pam continued to stand with the girls backstage, as they continued to watch the remainder of the contest. After each contestant walked the stage, the girls mingled talking backstage, with family, friends, and school staff.

Brooke's parents, along with her grandparents, joined her backstage, with Aunt Pam and Jill. Brooke explained to them what happened with her wig, and why she wore her natural hair, for the contest.

Brooke's mom in tears, hugged her daughter, constantly saying, how beautiful she was, and how proud she was of her and Jill.

Then Craig grabbed his daughter's hand, and looked into her eyes, and said, "You made me so proud, princess."

Brooke felt so overjoyed to receive the support from her family. But she felt in her heart she would not win.

Finally, after fifteen minutes of deliberation, the three judges, two who were school teachers, and one guest judge from a modeling agency, got the school's attention, and began to announce the second-place winner, and then the first-place winner.

One of the female teachers stated, "All of the girls did an amazing job, and looked stunning during this hair and beauty contest, but there is only one winner, and a runner-up, we thought was impressive, to the whole audience, not only for their beauty, but also their gracious character. The second-place winner, who was chosen to be the model of the year is... Ruth Wilson!"

Ruth looked shocked, and felt paralyzed for a moment, not believing she heard her name. Brooke jumped up with gladness, and yelled loudly, "Ruth, you won second place. Congratulations!"

Ruth walked up proudly to the stage, and she could see her parents cheering her on, as she was given a beautiful silver rose trophy.

The guest lady announcer from the modeling agency walked up to the stage, shook Ruth's hand, and said, "Congratulations," as Ruth greeted her with a "Thank you," and walked away.

"Drum roll please," said the guest announcer.

The guest announcer continued to say, "Not only is the beauty of the year considered a first-class winner, but she also demonstrates character of a true young lady, who displays beauty from the inside out, of kindness, bravery, and beauty to herself, and toward others, so the first-place winner is... Brooke Bell!"

Brooke's eyes were full of water. She looked at her parents and her aunt Pam and felt weak in shock, sobbing from her tears, asking in total shock,

"I won?"

The female announcer smiled graciously at Brooke, and beckoned for her to get her prize, of a beautiful shiny golden rose trophy, with a huge card board check $5000, one of the school teacher judges held, at the judging table not on stage.

As Brooke walked up to get her golden rose trophy first, her parents smiled at her, and the audience clapped loudly.

Ruth stood by, smiling and adoring Brooke, as she claimed her prizes.

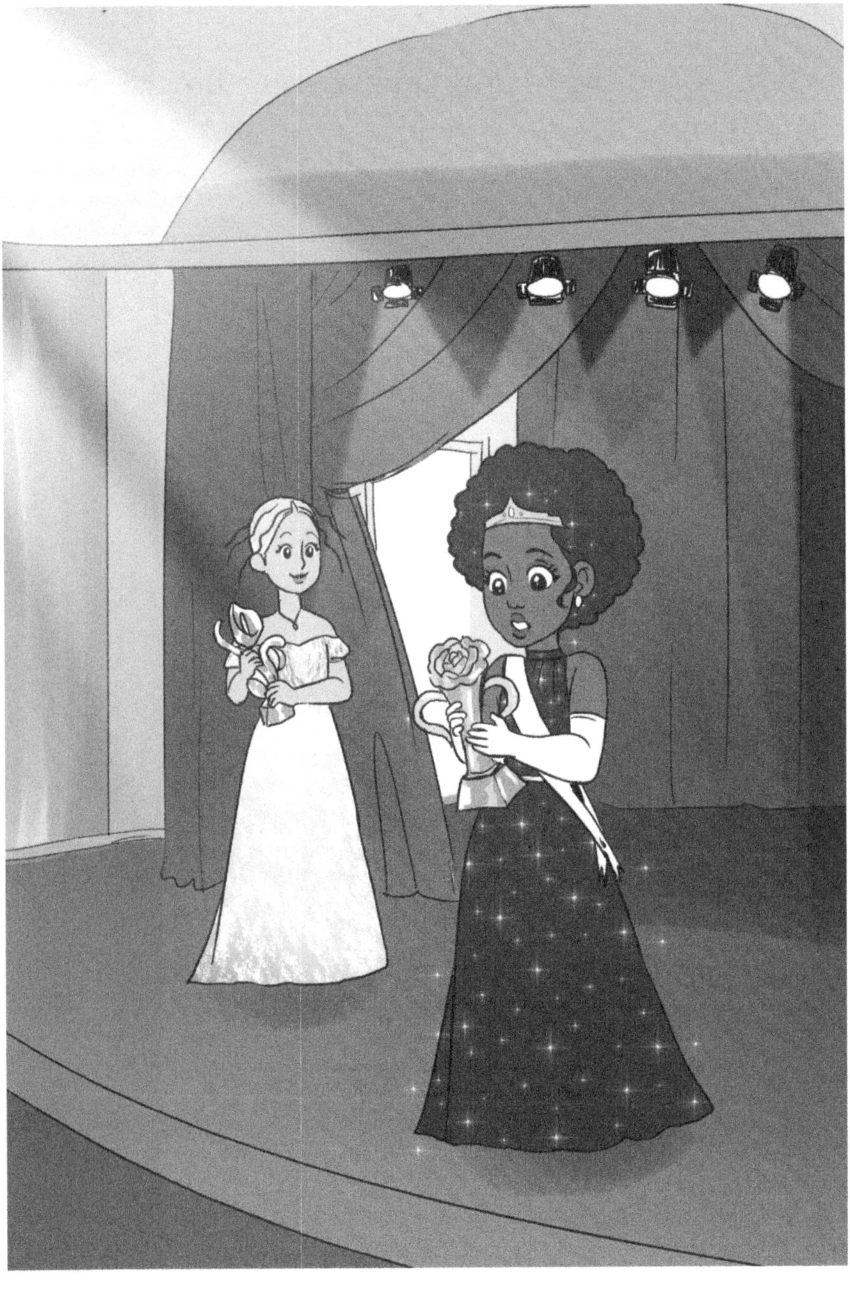

"Congratulations young lady," the female announcer said.

Brooke smiled, as she was given a microphone, and Brooke said, "I am so grateful to God, and my family, and I thank all of you in the audience." During this moment, thoughts of Brooke's *wonder wig*, raced through her mind, as she realized, she didn't need a wig, to feel beautiful inside or outside herself. Brooke knew this was a life-changing moment for her, and she worried about, how she would explain to her family later, what she discovered about her *wonder wig*.

In the meantime, Grandma Lu walked up to the stage to hug her granddaughter, and Brooke was so happy to hug her grandmother, as her parents, Aunt Pam, Jill, and Ruth joined her on stage.

After the beauty contest, Brooke had a wonderful time celebrating with her family, over a hearty home-cooked meal, at her parents' house. They all had an amazing time sharing their glazed roast chicken meal, admiring Brooke and Jill, and the second-place winner, Ruth, for doing a fine job modeling in the beauty contest. Although Ruth was not with them at the dinner table, Brooke was proud of her, and thought much about Ruth, as the evening was ending with her parents, and as she watched her grandparents, Aunt Pam, and Jill leave her parents' house, cheerfully for the night.

"We are so proud of you," Brooke's father said to her, as he gave her a tight embrace. Brooke smiled at her father.

Then Brooke's mother, Barb, walked over to Brooke, and gave her a kiss on her face cheek and said, "You were gorgeous!"

Brooke said with a smile, "Thank you Mom."

Brooke was overwhelmed with emotions of happiness and joy all at the same time because, it was one of the most perfect evenings she ever had, feeling beautiful about herself, and feeling loved by her family's support, and finally feeling a mother bond with her mom.

"Well, we are off to bed. Goodnight Brooke," her father said to her, with his arm around her mother's waist.

"Good night Dad," Brooke said.

"Good night baby," Brooke's mother said to her.

"Good night Mom," Brooke replied.

Brooke watched her parents go in their room and closed their door. Brooke then went into her room with racing thoughts pondering in her mind, what to do with her *wonder wig?* She did not know if she should keep it a secret, and continue to help other young girls with their alopecia, or if she should be like a Santa Claus, and leave gift bags or wigs at the desks of girl students, before they arrived to class, like a hero. Then, Brooke went to her hair drawer, and looked at the many bags of hair and weaves, and then she saw her *wonder wig*, buried under five hair bags. She thought to herself, that was how she mistakenly grabbed the wrong bag. She meant to put her *wonder wig* bag in a separate drawer shelf. However, she slowly opened her *wonder wig* bag, smiling and thinking, she didn't need the wig, to be a first-place winner in the beauty contest, and that people accepted her and her appearance for who she was, as a decent person.

Then Brooke slowly put the *wonder wig* on, looking carefully at herself in her vanity mirror. Suddenly, she could hear a young teen girl conversation with her mother, asking about her next dermatologist appointment, to have her hair scalp examined. She could hear the young girl weeping in tears, and the mother's voice comforting her. The mother said, "Nicole, don't cry." Then the voices faded away and stopped.

Brooke was overwhelmed about what she just heard, and her eyes swelled up with tears. It was like she could hear these voices over a radio system, that the *wonder wig* was allowing her to hear.

Then, Brooke sadly removed from her head, the *wonder wig.* Brooke felt compassion about helping others with hair care, and she felt an obligation to try to help the poor young girl she could hear weeping about her alopecia through the *wonder wig.* So Brooke was trying to determine the location of the voices. She felt she had to do something to help, but she did not want anyone to know. So she came up with a plan to buy a new wig, to get for the young teen girl, she could hear through the *wonder wig.* Brooke assumed the voices she heard, may have been at a nearby hair clinic. So Brooke looked on her computer, and researched the nearest dermatology clinic. She found one online about five blocks ways from her parents' house.

The next day was Saturday. As Brooke's dad was taking her to Aunt Pam's shop to work, Brooke noticed her dad driving by the hair clinic, and Brooke's eyes stared at the building as they drove by. Brooke finally arrived at Aunt Pam's hair salon. Brooke walked in the hair salon, anxious to talk to Aunt Pam later, about getting some new wigs. As soon as Brooke walked in the hair shop, she noticed the hair salon was very busy. Aunt Pam and Jill were happy to see Brooke. Brooke right away, put on her salon apron, and began to open new hair products to set on display for Aunt Pam's hair salon. Brooke also noticed seven new gorgeous different colored wigs on display. She really liked the blue, yellow, and pink wigs because, they were extravagant-looking and different. She quickly walked by the wigs on the manikins, and put her hands through the wigs hair. Brooke smiled. Jill noticed.

"Aren't they pretty?" Jill asked Brooke.

"Yes, I wonder if Aunt Pam will let me buy one on discount," Brooke asked Jill.

Then Jill looked puzzled at Brooke and asked, "You want another wig? I thought you didn't want to wear wigs anymore."

Brooke smirked and responded, "I never said I didn't want to wear wigs anymore altogether. I just didn't have need for one at the beauty contest."

When the hair shop finally is empty of clients, Aunt Pam paid Brooke and Jill $50 for their work. Brooke and Jill were happy as usual. Then Jill walked over to the television room and watched a cooking program.

Meanwhile, Brooke thought this was her chance to talk to her aunt Pam alone. She then asked Aunt Pam, "Aunt Pam, will it be okay if I purchased one of your new wigs?"

"Another wig?" Aunt Pam asked with amusement.

"Yes, I want to buy one, not for me, but for a friend."

"Okay, well, which one do you like?" Aunt Pam asked.

Brooke walked toward the wig displays, and she noticed a cute shoulder-length curly black wig. Brooke touched the black wig and said, "This one, Aunt Pam. How much?"

"Well, these are human-hair wigs, quite expensive, but for you, since you have worked so well in the shop, I will discount it to you as a gift for just $25."

Brooke's eyes brightened, as she smiled and handed her aunt Pam $25.

Her aunt Pam took the money, and wrapped the wig carefully in a bag. Brooke also saw a cute pair of black fashion diamond sunglasses.

"Can I buy these glasses too?" Brooke asked, smiling.

Aunt Pam replied, "Here, you can have these as a gift."

"Thank you so much Aunt Pam," Brooke stated happily.

"Now who is this special friend?" Aunt Pam asked suspiciously grinning.

"You never met her, but, Aunt Pam, this wig will look amazing on her."

"If you say so," Aunt Pam replied, smiling.

Brooke was happy, but trying to find a way to get the wig to the hair clinic, and to the right person. She felt it was almost impossible. But she believed if she could get it to the clinic, the wig would be of use to someone. Suddenly, Brooke decided to ask Aunt Pam, if she could call her dad, and ask for his permission, to walk to Grandma Lu's house, just ten blocks away from aunt Pam's hair shop.

Aunt Pam asked suspiciously, "Why?"

"I want the exercise," said Brooke hesitantly.

So Brooke called her dad's cell phone from the hair salon phone, and although he was confused about her wanting to walk to his parents' house, he gave her permission, and told her that, her mother would be picking her up at his parents' house in a few hours.

A few minutes later, Brooke left the hair salon, put on her coat, and her new black diamond fashion sunglasses, and began to walk with the new wig packed in a bag.

She wore the sunglasses because she admired the style, but she also planned not to be recognized by anyone at the hair clinic she was about to visit. She was enjoying the sunny weather and looked closely to the streets and signs, trying to find the hair clinic. After fifteen minutes of walking, she found it. She hurriedly walked into the hair clinic, nervously, asking the lady clerk for a nurse.

The lady clerk asked if Brooke had an appointment. After Brooke stated she did not have an appointment, Brooke waited in the lobby, for a nurse, to give the nurse a wig as a donation for a alopecia patient. After minutes of waiting, a lady nurse came to the lobby front desk, looking at Brooke, curious to the reason for her visit.

Brooke politely said to the nurse, "Hi. I don't have an appointment, but I was just wondering, does your clinic accept hair donations?"

The lady nurse looked astonished, but curious to why, a young lady Brooke's age, was asking this question.

"Why yes, you would have to complete a form, and tell us what you're donating," the nurse stated.

Brooke replied defensively, "No, I just want to donate this beautiful wig to one of your female patients. Don't know if someone named Nicole is here?"

The nurse gave a look of careful thinking and said, "Wait, there is a Nicole that was here yesterday, room 7, has another appointment tomorrow. That is very kind of you to want to give her a wig as a gift. Do you know her personally?" asked the lady nurse.

Brooke reluctantly said, "No, I just heard about her, and wanted to help her with her alopecia."

The lady nurse, and the desk clerk hearts were warmed with joy, from Brooke's kind gesture. Brooke then handed the wig to the lady nurse to look at the wig.

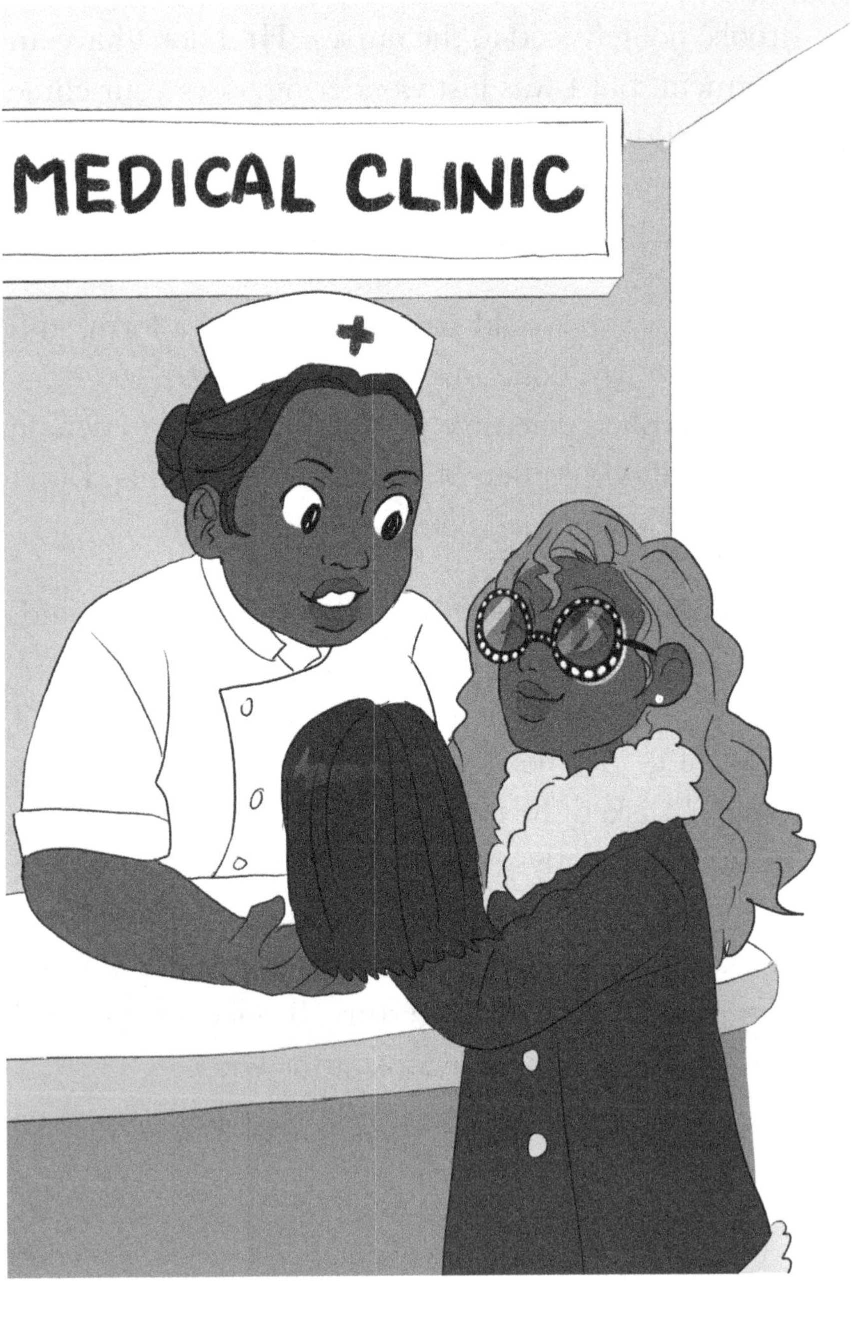
MEDICAL CLINIC

The lady nurse said, "It's stunning. Let me get you a form to write on, giving us your name."

"No, no, that's okay. If you can give this to her?" Brooke asked.

"Sure thing," the lady nurse replied.

Brooke smiled and replied, "Thank you."

As Brooke tried to walk away fast, the lady nurse said, "Wait, what is your name?"

Brooke waved at the lady nurse, and walked out of the clinic in a hurry. Brooke's heart was beating fast, but she was relieved and proud of herself because, she was able to leave the clinic, without her identity being revealed. So Brooke continued on toward her grandparent's house, and finally arrived there.

Grandma Lu embraced her, after she walked in the house, and was looking at Brooke, amused about her new sunglasses.

"What's this new look I see?" Grandma Lu asked Brooke.

Brooke smirked at her grandmother and asked, "Do you like them, Grandma Lu? Aren't they adorable?" Then Brooke removed her sunglasses.

"They are dazzling, and how has your day been? Are you staying out of mischief?" Grandma Lu asked, chuckling.

Brooke looked dumbfounded and said, "I just decided to walk to your house to get some fresh air."

"You walked?" Grandma Lu asked in shock.

"Yes Grandma, I am all right."

"I was wondering why your aunt Pam didn't bring you by today?"

"I asked aunt Pam and Dad, if I could walk to your house, and it was alright with them."

"Okay, but where is your new wig?" Grandma Lu asked with curiosity.

"My new wig? How did you know?" Brooke asked with surprise.

"Your aunt Pam told me you bought a cute little wig, but she didn't tell me she wasn't bringing you here. So where is it?" Grandma Lu asked, demanding to know.

Brooke felt nervous, and didn't know how she would answer her grandmother. She didn't want to lie, but she didn't know how to explain to her where she was.

Brooke looked into her Grandma Lu's eyes, and did not want to tell her a lie, so she explained to her how she took a wig to the hair clinic as a gift, but she did not tell her about her *wonder wig,* and its power, to reveal to her, people who had alopecia.

"Hmmm, well, that was a real kind thing you did, but what made you go give them a wig?" Grandma Lu asked, handing Brooke a glass of iced lemonade.

Brooke took a sip of her lemonade then replied, "I wanted to do something nice for people with alopecia, just like Ruth at my school, who won second place in the beauty contest."

That is so generous of you Brooke. I am so proud of you. It is important to give to others, who don't have basic things, and I think, whoever gets the wig, will be grateful," Grandma Lu replied.

Brooke, with a half grin, said, "I hope so." Then Brooke tried to change the subject, but also wondered, if she could trust her Grandma Lu with her secret about the *wonder wig*.

Grandma Lu sensed Brooke was acting unusual, and asked her, "You alright? Is there something you want to talk to your Granny Lu about?"

Just as Brooke was about to tell her grandmother Lu her secret about the *wonder wig*, Grandpa Dale interrupted their conversation, asking for dinner.

Brooke then lost the courage to tell her grandmother Lu.

Grandma Lu said to Grandpa Dale, "It is almost ready." Grandma Lu said to Brooke, "We will continue our talk later."

Then Grandma Lu began to fix Grandpa Dale a plate of chicken and macaroni and cheese meal.

Brooke took her glass of lemonade, a piece of her grandmother's homemade German chocolate cake on a small saucer, and cautiously walked to the dining room, to read a hair magazine, while enjoying her cake, and lemonade at the dining room table.

That evening, Barb arrived outside to pick up Brooke. Brooke said her goodbyes to her grandparents for the day, and met her mom in her truck.

Brooke's mother noticed Brooke carrying diamond sunglasses in her hand.

"How was your day baby?" Brooke's mother asked.

"It was nice Mom, and yours?"

"Busy at the shop as usual," Brooke's mom replied. "I heard you walked to your grandparents' house. Your dad told me on the phone. Any special reason? Everything okay with your aunt Pam?" Barb asked with concern.

"No, everything is fine Mom, I just wanted to walk. The exercise was good for me," Brooke said.

"Well, you know, if you worked for me, you would be closer to walking home than to your grandparents'," Barb said strategically, trying to convince Brooke to work with her part time as well. So just before they arrived home, Barb thought it would be a good time to ask Brooke about working for her part time at her shop because, Barb was so proud of her daughter and felt their relationship was healing, since the beauty contest, and how well their friendship had grown. So Barb decided to propose a paid-job offer to Brooke, and asked her if she would be interested in alternating her Saturday workdays, to work with her one Saturday, and at her aunt Pam's the alternate Saturday.

Brooke paused for a minute, and thought about her conversation with Grandma Lu's years ago, about the importance of a mother-and-daughter relationship, and how protective mothers are of their daughters, who they want the best for, just like her grandmother Lu and aunt Pam.

Barb then said, "You would be closer to home on Saturdays, on some of your walks from my shop, if you needed to go home, when I am still at my hair shop."

Brooke smiled at her mom and said, "Sure Mom, that would be nice for us to work closer together, and a nice change of scenery for me. I will let Aunt Pam know."

Barb felt so excited, and hugged her daughter saying, "Thank you. It will be fun, and I will let your dad know, and I will also talk to your aunt Pam as well."

"Sounds good Mom, and I will start in a few weeks, just to give Aunt Pam time to adjust, not having my help as much," Brooke said.

So, for the next few weeks, Brooke continued to put on her *wonder wig*, in private at home, listening in on conversations of different young girls, she knew of from her school, and the hair clinic. Another time, Brooke saved her money from her aunt Pam, and one week purchased five brown, black, and yellow wigs from her aunt Pam at a discounted price.

Aunt Pam and Jill were suspicious, but assumed Brooke loved wigs, and was buying them for herself.

However, Brooke a few times, walked to the hair clinic, with a bag of wigs, and left three at the counter, concealing her identity, remaining nameless.

Then one day, her Grandma Lu, was watching the news on television, and she saw a news report of recognition, of a nameless person, donating wigs to the hair clinic for girls with alopecia. They considered this act of kindness heroic, giving one a nickname as, *Dashing Dazzle*. The news reporter requested the person responsible, reveal herself, for a generous cash reward of $20,000 as a humanity award.

Grandma Lu was shocked almost out of her mind because, she had an inkling, it was her granddaughter Brooke because, of their recent conversation, about her walking to the clinic to donate a wig, and her kindness to her classmate, who won second place in the beauty contest.

Grandma Lu did not want to act in haste. So she waited later that day, until Brooke walked to her home.

Brooke finally got there that Saturday evening.

"Hi Grandma Lu," Brooke said with cheer, as she walked into her house.

"Well, young lady, good to see you. We need to talk," Grandma Lu said with firmness.

"Something wrong, Grandma Lu?" Brooke asked, feeling concerned.

Grandma Lu smiled, but then gave Brooke a sneaky look, and asked,

"Have you been donating more wigs to people?"

Brooke gave her grandmother a blank stare, and she felt speechless.

"Come on child, tell me, is this you?" Grandma Lu asked anxiously.

"Yes Grandma Lu, that is what I was trying to tell you the other week, but Grandpa was ready for dinner, and we never finished talking about it," Brooke replied, then continued, "How did you find out? How do you know?

"Child, I saw a news reporter today on television, speak about a mystery person donating wigs, and they want to reward this person $20,000, and they called the young lady, *Dashing Dazzle*," Grandma Lu whispered.

Brooke's jaw dropped on her face. Brooke was completely shocked. She did not want to reveal who she was, but she wanted the reward. She was thinking, the money could help her pay her college tuition, to go to beauty school, to become a hairstylist, or to donate the money to an organization for women and girls with alopecia. She also wanted to buy a nice silver car to travel, to make it easier for her to continue to anonymously, make her wig donations. Although Brooke was ready to reveal herself as the mystery wig giver, she was not ready to reveal the *wonder wig* to a soul.

Grandma Lu stated, "I suppose they saw your blinging glasses, and gave you the nick name, *Dashing Dazzle*. That is so adorable, Brooke. Are you going to tell your folks, or do I need to tell them for you?"

Brooke was excited and conflicted about her being recognized publicly as a hero, and she knew she had to make a decision fast. Brooke looked at her grandmother in silence, confused on what to do.

"Brooke, baby, what are you going to do? You are being honored in a special way, and you should not be ashamed, but proud to help your community, and help those in need of decent hair care. I am honored to be your grandmother, and I am very proud of you," Grandma Lu stated.

Brooke said to her grandmother, "Thank you, Grandma Lu. Yes, I will tell Dad and Mom as soon as I can."

"Girl, you better tell them today, before they hear it on the news themselves," Grandma Lu replied.

"Grandma, Dad and Mom barely watch the news. They are usually too tired from work to watch the news. But Dad reads the newspaper a lot. Will it be in the newspaper, Grandma Lu?" Brooke asked nervously.

"Well, I don't know. I better buy a paper at the market place tomorrow and check. In the meantime, you better find a way quickly, to tell your parents, and be happy about your recognition. There is nothing to be afraid of or ashamed of, Brooke."

"Yeah, I guess you are right, Grandma Lu," Brooke replied.

So Brooke spent an hour watching the news on television, trying to see if they were covering her wig stories, until her dad was to meet Brooke at her grandma Lu's, to take her home. As Brooke sat on her grandmother's sofa, she was trying to decide how to tell her parents, without revealing her *wonder wig*. She still was not ready to reveal that, and she felt she needed more time to wait, so that when she finally tells them, they would not be angry with her for not telling them about her *wonder wig* before. She did not want her parents, not to trust her.

The Wonder Wig

When Brooke got home that night, she did not want to put on her *wonder wig* that night. She was afraid, that her parents would catch her wearing it in her room, so she decided to keep it under lock and key, out of sight, until she had devised a new plan on how to tell them, about her giving away wigs to many girls, like Ruth, with alopecia. As the night continued, Brooke would peek into the living room, to see if her parents were watching the news, but her dad just surfed the television stations, skipping over the news. Brooke was mentally on edge, while still thinking of creative ways, how to continue to help girls and women with alopecia, whom she cared for from her heart. But now, the news media was distracting her from continuing her good deeds, and she stopped going to hair clinics temporarily, to avoid being harassed by paparazzi and the news.

Brooke was almost holding her breath, as she struggled to find a way to tell her family about her *wonder wig*, and to reveal to the public, she was mystery wig shero, to be honored and be rewarded.

A couple days later, on Monday morning, when Brooke got to school, her friend Ruth asked to speak with her alone.

"Hi Ruth, What's going on? Everything alright?" Brooke asked with concern.

Ruth whispered, "Hey girly, no everything is fine, just wondering, did you see the news yesterday, about a mystery lady donating wigs to the medical clinic for girls and women with alopecia? Are you *Dashing Dazzle?*"

Brooke smiled and replied, "Yes, it's me, but I didn't want the whole world to know."

Ruth jumped for joy, hugged Brooke, and said, "I knew it! You are a beautiful person. I am just amazed at how selfless you are, helping me and others without wanting recognition, and you give from your heart. So what are you going to do? You have to reveal yourself, and there is a money reward of $20,000!" Ruth said.

Brooke replied, "I know. I will need to talk to my family first. Then I will go public."

Ruth hugged Brooke again with excitement, saying, "Your secret is safe with me."

Brooke looked at Ruth with gratitude and said, "Thank you. I will let you know what happens. Talk to you again soon."

CHAPTER 7

The Wonder Wig Revealed

The next day, after school, Brooke decided to surprise her mom, and work at her salon, *That Look,* during the week day on Tuesday. That particular day, a special new client with alopecia stopped in, asking for Brooke's mother help with her hair. Brooke watched closely, how her mother Barb, showed kindness and sensitivity to the lady client, and they had a conversation about her hair disease. The customer explained, it started from childbirth, and how she struggled with her self-esteem for many years. The client was about fifty years of age, and as Barb examined her hair, delicately combing through it, she showed her client magazines of hairstyles, she could give her, to help brighten her spirit. Brooke felt compassion for the client, and she realized, she did not need her *wonder wig,* to know about her alopecia story.

As Brooke was dusting and sweeping the floors of her mother's salon, she eagerly eavesdropped to the client's story of her struggle with unexplained hair loss being genetic, and her questions on how to grow her hair. Brooke was impressed with how her mother spent time, trying to help the lady client with alopecia. Brooke listened to her mother comfort the client with her words of encouragement, calling her beautiful, as she offered her client help with her hair care, to give her the option of a unique natural hair style, or the client choosing one of the salon wigs of her choice, for her client to continue to feel beautiful. Her mother gently combed the client's hair, showing her different styles with a black hand mirror, and the client smiled with hope. Barb then took her client to a shampoo bowl and gave her hair a good wash, shampoo, and conditioning through the bare scalp parts of her hair. Afterward, she towel-dried her hair, and used low heat to comb-dry through client's hair. Then Barb asked the client if she wanted a press-and-curl hairstyle or a wig? The client wanted both.

So Barb moisturized client's hair scalp with Mielle hair oil, and gave her client, beautiful small Shirley-Temple curls with bangs on her face. Brooke was mesmerized about the Shirley Temple curls hairstyle on her mother's client's hair. Brooke admired, how her mother transformed the lady's hair. The bald parts of her scalp were not visible. Brooke's eyes were in tears. She felt such compassion for the client, and she was so impressed with her mom's skills to beautify women's hair.

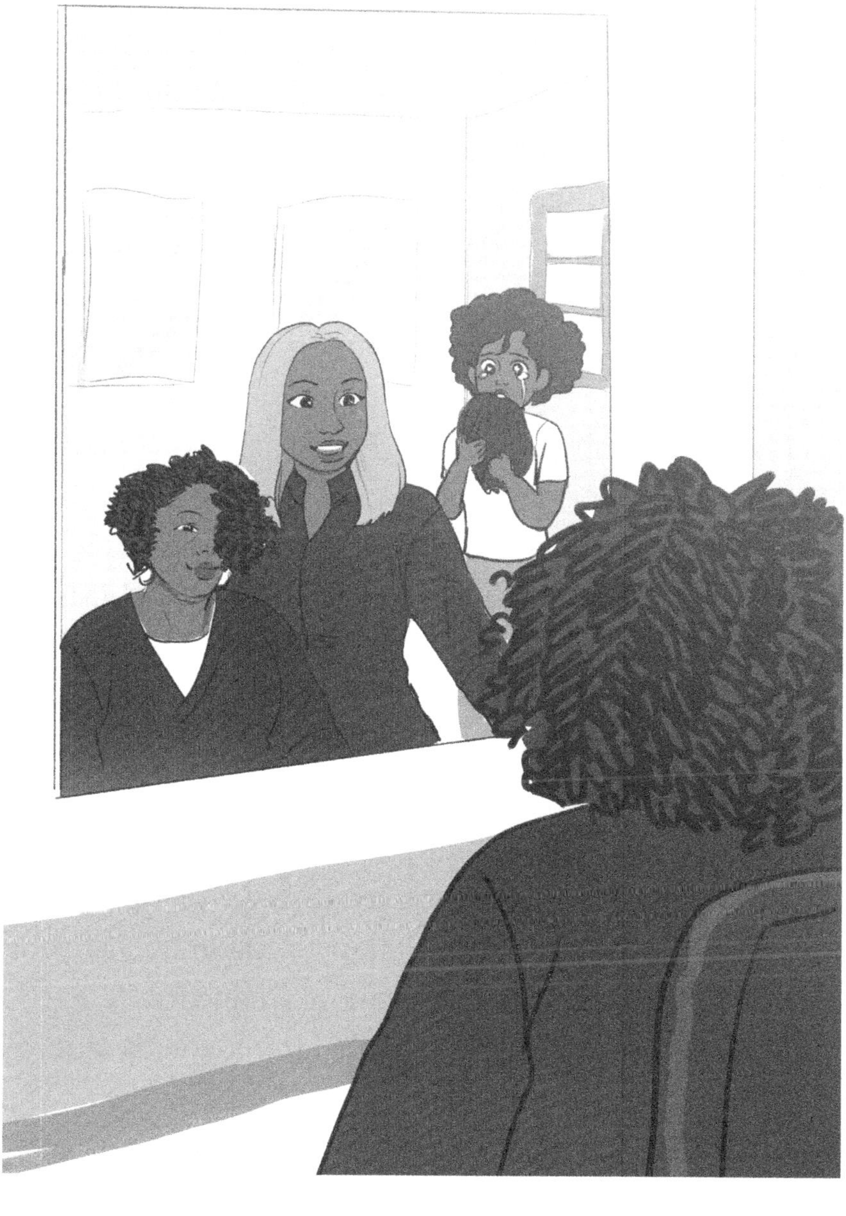

Thank you so much Mrs. Barb, my hair looks lovely, and I feel gorgeous," the lady client said.

As Barb was removing her client's apron and brushing hair from her client's apron, Brooke smiled at the client, with no words, and began to sweep the hair salon floor. Then the client went over to the display counter of wigs, and chose a short wavy burgundy wig, and brought it over to Barb, stating, "This one is so beautiful, I will pay for this with my hair care fee as well, and I will wear this wig after this hairstyle wears off."

Barb smiled and said, "Yes, that is one of my favorite wigs."

The client smiled and paid Barb cash money for her hair care service.

As the client left her chair, she said, "Mrs. Barb, you do amazing work. I will be back. Can I have a business card to schedule another appointment soon?"

"Sure. Brooke, hand her a business card," Barb asked.

Brooke was happy to get her mother's business card, and handed it to her client.

As her client was walking to the hair shop door to leave, Barb stated, "Don't forget to try rice water hair products on your scalp and hair. That may help for treatment, and grow your hair more frequently."

The client smiled. "Yes, I will. Thank you, and have a good day."

Barb waved at the client as she left the hair salon.

Barb sat in her shop chair, took a deep breath, looked at Brooke, and smiled. Brooke smiled at her mother, feeling proud of her.

Brooke then said, "Mom, that woman you helped today looked so beautiful, and I thought you did a great job with counseling her and making her feel pretty and look pretty."

Barb felt good in her heart to hear her daughter admire her work. Because of their past distant relationship, she never shared her thoughts about her work before. Barb was so happy her daughter was with her, and she said, "Just like you helped your schoolmate, such a wonderful thing to do. You know, Brooke, I know you would be a great hairstylist."

At this moment, Brooke pondered telling her mom her secret about the *wonder wig*, her mystery wig donations, and the public rumor about her. So finally, Brooke decided to tell her secret to her mother, about her mysterious *wonder wig*.

"What? Brooke, are you serious? The wig from Aunt Pam's shop has special powers?" Brooke's mother asked in shock.

In tears, Brooke responded, "Yes Mom, and I didn't know how to tell anyone because, I was going through my own insecurities. You and I weren't that close. Dad would always tell me, I am beautiful no matter what, but not really understand the emotions a woman struggles with inside her mind. Grandma Lu was so comfortable to talk to, and what is so funny, she suspected something going on with me from the day of the beauty contest."

Brooke's mother chuckled. "So your father doesn't know. Are you sure no one else knows?" Barb asked.

"Ruth knows about me being the mystery donor of wigs to a few students at school, and the health clinic, but she doesn't know my *wonder wig* has special powers. That's how I knew to help her, and I gave her a wig, weeks before the beauty contest."

"Wow Brooke, this is weird, but amazing at the same time. You really are like a hero, *Ms. Dashing Dazzle*" Brooke's mother said with joy.

"I am so relieved I am not carrying this secret by myself anymore Mom, and I am so glad you didn't judge me for not telling right away," Brooke said to her mom.

"No baby, to find a wig that gives you the ability to hear conversations of people with alopecia is just, just, just . . . We got to tell your father. I can't wait to see this wig!" Brooke's mother said cheerfully.

"I know, then I need to tell Aunt Pam, Grandpa Dale, and then the news reporter," Brooke replied.

"Well, let's get going to go tell your dad, and we will call the family over for a meeting, to discuss, and make arrangements with the media for tomorrow," Barb stated to her daughter Brooke.

So Brooke left the hair salon with her mother to meet her dad at home to break the news to him about her *wonder wig.* When they finally arrived home, Brooke could see her dad reading the newspaper with a photo of her with sunglasses. The newspaper stated, "God bless the mystery wig lady, *Dashing Dazzle,* for giving to the needy, for patients with alopecia. Please reveal yourself. You deserve a humanitarian award. We are grateful to you."

Barb looked at her daughter Brooke, suspiciously wondering if Brooke's dad had already figured out who the mystery giver was.

"Hi ladies!" Craig said to his wife Barb, and then to his daughter Brooke, as he held the newspaper grinning, looking at Brooke cautiously, as if he knew she had been up to something, and she was the mystery person, giving away wigs, to help those with alopecia.

Barb looked at her husband and asked, "Craig, what do you know?"

Brooke was sweating, and feeling somewhat nervous, but eager to hear her dad's response. Brooke's dad continued to stare at her, while holding up the front page of the paper, and her dad asked with a look of surprise, "Is this you, young lady?"

Brooke looked worried and grinned, stating, "Yes, Daddy. How did you know?"

Smiling, Brooke's dad responded by saying, "Well, I remember these sunglasses."

Barb said happily, "Craig, isn't this news shocking and amazing at the same time?"

He smiled and said, "Yes, this seems absolutely unbelievable, and amazing all at the same time."

Brooke looked at her mom. They both knew, there was more to tell him about her *wonder wig*.

Brooke then hesitantly said, "Dad, there is one more thing to tell you."

Barb smirked, and gave Brooke a look with her eyes, directing her to go to her room to get the *wonder wig*, her mother was so anxious to see, before Brooke continued to unveil her story.

"What is it?" Craig looked at Barb with curiosity.

Barb said, "Wait . . . I want her to tell you."

Barb was already waiting anxiously, to examine Brooke's *wonder wig*. Then Brooke, with her *wonder wig*, slowly walked back into the living room, where her parents were. Brooke's father was eager to see what Brooke was holding in her hand. As Brooke walked toward her parents, with the *wonder wig*, the wig glowed and glistened with beauty. Then Brooke handed the wig to her mother to look at, as her father watched. Barb was putting her fingers through the wig's hair strands, looking thoroughly at the wig, and under the wig. Barb was smiling, but wondering where the super powers were?

Brooke paused, to reveal to her father, the super powers of her wig, as Brooke watched her mother carefully put the wig on.

Brooke was curious to see if her mother would hear the conversations of alopecia patients, or other people suffering from the disease.

Brooke's mother put on the wig, trying to tune in to anything unusual she could hear, and she could hear nothing.

"Hmm," Barb said to Brooke, Brooke was completely surprised, and wondering, why her mother could not hear any voices from the wig?

Meanwhile, Craig was still waiting for his daughter to explain what was so peculiar about her wig.

"What is it Brooke?" her dad asked again with eagerness.

"Dad, months ago, I discovered that my wig, had special power, and I kept it a secret because, it was overwhelming to me, and I didn't know how to tell you and Mom at first."

"Wow, really?" her father replied.

Brooke then tried on the wig, and immediately, heard an unfamiliar voice, of a woman talking to another woman about her alopecia.

"I can hear, I can hear these ladies talking!" Brooke shouted to her parents, and she snatched off her wig, and handed her *wonder wig*, to her mom again to try on wig and to listen.

Barb put the wig on tightly, and she couldn't hear a thing.

"I can't hear anything?" Barb said, looking dumbfounded to Brooke.

Brooke's mother handed the wig back to her, and Brooke tried on the *wonder wig*, again, and immediately, she heard ladies talking about their hair scalps. Brooke was puzzled about why she could only hear the voices.

Brooke said worriedly, "Mom, I don't understand, I am telling you the truth, I can hear women talking.

That is how I was able to help my friend Ruth at school, by giving her a wig as a gift, and other people at the dermatologist clinics."

Barb said, "I believe you baby. The wig may only work for you because, it is your special work in life, to help people with alopecia."

Brooke's father chimed in and said with amusement, "Young lady, you mean to tell me, you been secretly giving away wigs to other students at school, and the medical clinic all this time?"

Brooke gave a half grin, looking at her father with a shy look, and said, "Yes."

"So this is why, people are calling you, *Dashing Dazzle?*"

Suddenly, Brooke's dad jumped up, and took the *wonder wig* from Brooke, looking at it with amazement, smiling. Then he shook the wig, and put the wig to one of his ears.

Barb and Brooke laughed at Craig because, he looked silly shaking the wig, as it lit up, and the wig kept flashing, like a Christmas tree. Then Brooke's father discovered, he could not hear anything either from the *wonder wig*, and he slowly handed Brooke's special wig back to her.

"Does my parents know or anyone else?" Brooke's dad asked.

Brooke said, "Grandma Lu only knows about me giving away wigs, but not about my *wonder wig.*"

"The what?" Brooke's dad asked with amusement.

"My wig. I call it, the *wonder wig*," Brooke stated, grinning.

"That's a cool name," Brooke's dad replied.

"So, what are we going to do about telling the family, and then talking to the media?" Barb asked her husband Craig.

Craig paused, and then looked at this wife, and his daughter Brooke, and said, "Let's have a family dinner Friday, and have Brooke tell them."

Brooke looked at her parents happily and said, "Yes, that would be great."

Friday finally arrived, and Craig's parents showed up first. Craig, Barb, and Brooke greeted them, with hugs, and seated them at the dining room table, giving them appetizers of crackers, cheese, broccoli, and pepperoni sausage, with pineapple juice to snack on. Grandma Lu was smirking at Brooke at the table, because she knew the meeting was going to be about Brooke being discovered as a wig giver and shero.

Grandpa Dale asked with amusement, "So what is this get-together all about?"

Craig said, "Dad, we have a star in our house, and we want to introduce this special person to our family." Barb and Brooke smirked at each other. Grandma Lu smiled at her son Craig.

A minute later, Pam arrived with Jill, and Brooke was so happy to see them as family, all greet one another with hugs.

Barb said, "Attention, I am so glad all of you could make it. We wanted you all to gather here obviously, to see one another, but to also share a special announcement."

Brooke went to her room, and quickly grabbed her special bag, hiding her *wonder wig*. Then she walked back into the dining room, and her grandparents and Aunt Pam and Jill were looking at her, puzzled about the bag. Then Brooke slowly pulled out the *wonder wig*. Aunt Pam smiled because, she recognized it, giving it to Brooke a while back.

Aunt Pam immediately said, "Look at that cute thing. You wearing it for a special occasion?"

"Yes Aunt Pam, I always appreciated you giving this special wig to me, and it is very special because for months, I did not tell you, or anyone, that it has . . . special powers," Brooke said with a spooky tone.

"What!" Aunt Pam shouted with surprise. Her brother Craig looked at his sister Pam, nodding to affirm Brooke was telling the truth.

Barb interrupted and said, "Yes Pam, she just revealed this to us after months of keeping it a secret, but Brooke will explain more."

"Brooke, you sneaky thing, well, what does it do?" Grandpa Dale asked with amusement, as he chuckled.

Brooke reluctantly said, "Well, whenever I put it on, I can mysteriously hear voices of women and girls talking about their hair troubles, particularly alopecia. That is how I was able to help my schoolmate, Ruth, with her hair before the beauty contest. Remember, she stopped using the wig I gave her during the beauty contest because, she knew I had decided to wear my natural short hair, and not cover it up, with no wig, during the beauty contest."

"Yes!" Aunt Pam said with excitement.

"Wow! That is why that one day, you were being weird, and protective at Mom's hair shop because, Mom gave you a wig with super powers, way cool!" Jill shouted.

Brooke smiled at Jill and nodded yes.

Grandma Lu chimed in and said, "So she is the young lady the news media has been talking about to reward because, of her special contributions to her schoolmates, and mostly at the dermatologist clinics; just amazing."

Aunt Pam's eyes began to tear up, as she looked at Barb, who also looked emotional.

Then Aunt Pam said, "So all those times you were buying extra wigs, were to help people with alopecia, Brooke?"

Brooke, looking at her aunt Pam, bashfully smiled and said, "Yes, that was why, Aunt Pam."

Aunt Pam rushed over to hug her niece and said, "Sweetie, I am sooo proud of you. Why didn't you say something?"

"I didn't know what to say. I was completely shocked out of my mind that this special wig had these powers. It was too overwhelming to talk about, and I just wanted to help those who needed help with their hair, the same way you and Mom help women all the time," Brooke expressed sympathetically.

"We are so proud of her, and now we must reveal to the public on the news, who Brooke is to the world!" Brooke's dad said proudly.

Barb began to slowly clap her hands in recognition of her daughter, and Brooke's family all began to clap their hands for her together.

Aunt Pam grabbed the wig from Brooke and examined it closely, smiling.

Barb then said, "We are scheduling an appointment with the press to share Brooke's story."

Brooke stated, "But, I only want to tell them I am the mystery girl, but not about my *wonder wig*."

Grandma Lu smiled and said, "Good idea. They don't need to know all the details. Who knows, Pam may have another stash of special wigs we don't know about?" The family all laughed.

"Can we agree on keeping this family secret?" Craig asked the family.

Everyone said together, "Yes." Brooke's family applauded her again. Brooke was overwhelmed with joy, happy to feel the support of her family.

Afterward, Jill walked over by her mom to look at the wig, when Brooke noticed her Mom and Aunt Pam were beginning a peaceful conversation. So that evening, Brooke enjoyed a special steak and potato meal, her dad cooked up to share with her family, and she was happy, her secret was finally out about her special wig, and she no longer felt alone or burdened with hiding her *wonder wig*.

Brooke's parents, grandparents, and Aunt Pam were just stunned, as well as impressed with Brooke's big heart, and public recognition, to help many people heal psychologically, from their hair troubles, offering a gift of hope and personal fashion to various patients lives, one by one, young and elderly.

Later that week, Brooke went to one of the local news stations, to talk to the leading reporter, and she revealed, she was, indeed, *Dashing Dazzle.*

The news reporter was excited to record Brooke, while she told her story about donating the wigs, but not about the *wonder wig.*

The next day, a news brief was held at one of the local television stations, and dozens of reporters from different stations crowded Brooke and her parents with microphones, and questions about her mystery deliveries of wigs. But Brooke never revealed to the news press, when, and how, she knew where to deliver the wigs. Brooke was going to keep this a secret between her and her family forever.

What is more, the television station gave a special gift to Brooke for her humanitarian services toward the medical and health community. As a reward, they gifted her a dazzling, shimmering black leather onesie suit costume, covered with real diamonds, for her new superhero look. This outfit was sophisticated and classic, which matched Brooke's sunglasses. She was also gifted the $20,000, and a surprised silver Chevy Malibu car, a car she always wanted.

As time went on, Brooke's mother continued to help supply Brooke with new wigs, to continue to give away to schools, medical clinics, and at her mother's beauty shop for girls and women suffering from Alopecia.

Later in life, Brooke went to a hair school to get her beautician degree. Although she earned her hair license and could have owned her own hair salon, she chose not to be tied to a hair salon. Instead, Brooke chose to start making and designing her own wigs, and became a high fashioned wigologist, to help donate countless wigs to give to her Mother's and her Aunt Pam's hair salons regularly, and to also help support some of their clients, who struggled with alopecia, or just wanted a new look to feel beautiful as young ladies or women. She also dedicated her life's work, traveling, as *Ms. Dashing Dazzle*, going to different cities and countries, hair salons, and medical clinics, delivering her own specialized wigs she made and designed to beauty shops and dermatologist clinics across the world.

Brooke's *wonder wig*, continued to notify her of many places to travel to, and help hair salons and dermatologist clinics that were in need of wigs. She would secretly drop off the wigs at reception desks without saying a word. There were also times, Brooke did not wear her *wonder wig*, and she would still provide hair wigs as gifts to many and people at public parks, not just hair salons and doctor offices. Many of the dermatologist doctors and hairstylists would try to start a conversation with her, as they recognized, she was one of the world's greatest of beauties, as *Dashing Dazzle*, who had the ability to walk in different places quickly, leaving beautiful gift bags, filled with all varieties of colors of hair wigs, weaves of different hair textures, of gorgeous styles. This made Brooke happy inside of her soul. Because she enjoyed, helping so many girls and women look and feel beautiful from her gift of wigs. This was a priceless service, Brooke would always cherish, to help others. Brooke's kind heart helped to build self-esteem and healed millions of people, not just locally, but across the world.

When she would come home to visit her family—her parents, grandparents, and Aunt Pam—she would share stories of her adventures, how she helped millions of people with makeover hairstyles, bringing them joy and a new confidence she was so proud to give to the world.

One time, Brooke's mom went to special fabric and jewelry stores, to choose a new costume for her, that was similar to the one she wore, but her new costume her mom designed for her, was more shiny and dazzling than the first. Brooke was grateful, and to go with her suit, she added a new pair of black fine diamond blinging sunglasses.

Another time, Brooke was in town, visiting her parents, Brooke shared with her family, a new beau she had met, who appeared to have the same mission to help people with alopecia, except he bought taupes for young boys and men, but didn't know how to gift them to others, nor did he possess any special powers as Brooke, to deliver them.

Brooke's mom asked, "So who is this special man you met, and will you tell him your secret about you being, *Dashing Dazzle*?"

Looking at her parents, Brooke smiled, paused and said, "Well, you all will just have to wait and see."

They all laughed and huddled together in the movie room of Brooke's parents home, enjoying hot salted popcorn, and a cold glass of lemonade. They were to watch a good wholesome family movie. This was exciting to Brooke. She spent family time with her parents whenever she could, always making the best of that time, until she planned for her next adventure, as *Dashing Dazzle*.

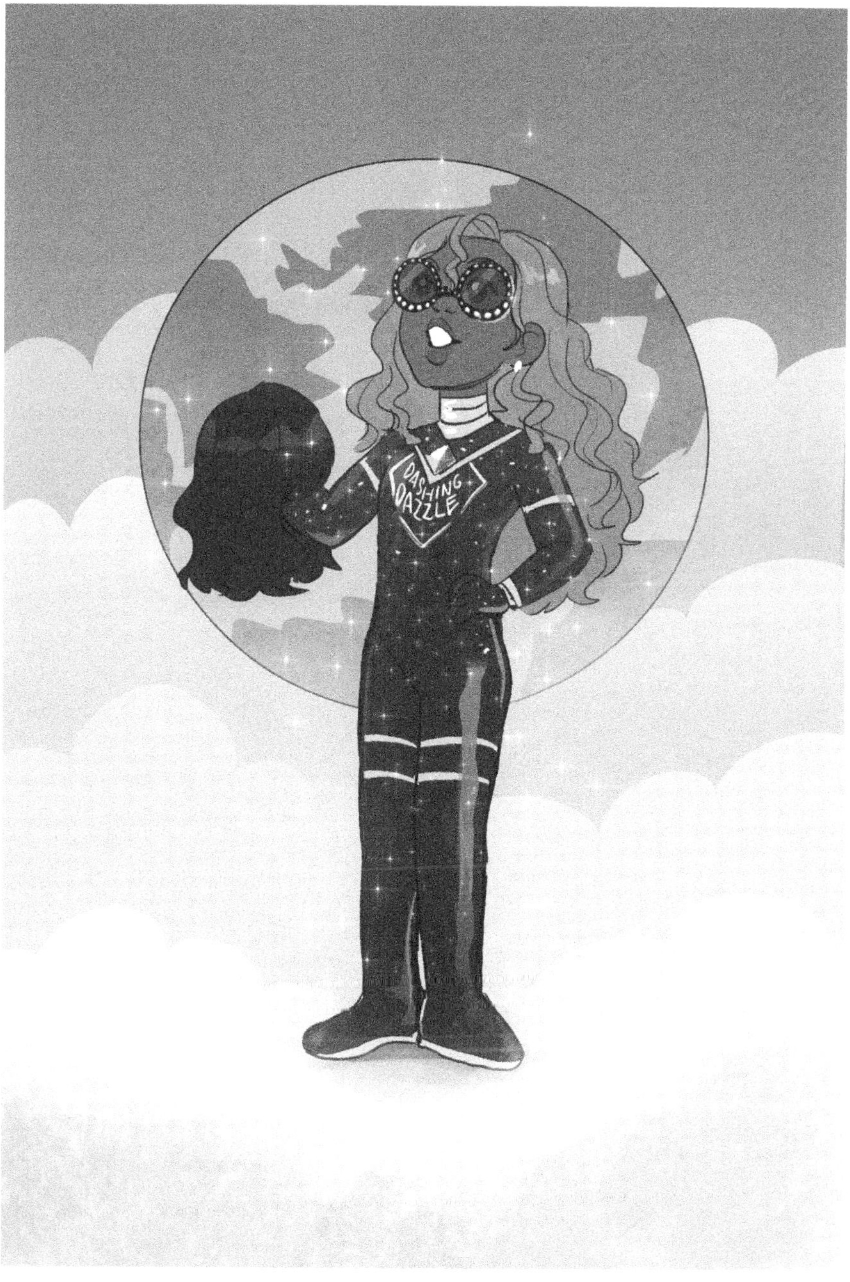
DASHING
DAZZLE

About the Author

I am an author of several inspirational books, a community wellness leader, a professional life coach, and an inspirational speaker. My gift of writing, came from God, and began developing at one of my childhood favorite elementary schools,I attended in the 80's, named, Golda Meir School for the Gifted and Talented, in Milwaukee Wisconsin.

Over the years, I have inspired people with my books and speeches for community wellness, how to live their best life. In my journey of living, I have experienced many challenges and adversities over the years, from my teen years through my adulthood. Sometimes life would seem so dark and overwhelming. However, overtime, I had to learn how to overcome hardships. I learned life is a gift, and I am to treasure it and to make the best of it, because life can get better if you choose to make it better. I also believe I have helped inspire many people about healthy living through my inspirational messages, my words of encouragement about the gift of life from the Creator, Almighty God, who gives abundance in life and purpose for humanity.

In 2018, I had my own personal hair journey of going from perm hair to natural, and I struggled with a new self-image, from long perm hair to short hair. I even had areas of my hair that was bald, and I had to learn to love myself and my new image. Therefore, I have recently developed an interest for advocacy regarding women's and young girl's health and self-image, appreciating who they are naturally, including their hair care for hair styling, whether it be their own hair, wigs, weaves, or extensions. I believe women and girls should embrace their beauty and feel good about themselves and how they look.

Therefore, my heartwarming fiction novel *The Wonder Wig* is a tale about a young girl, who learns to embrace her beauty, particularly her self-image, as she learns, the importance of hair care, but great character is more important. She later, becomes an advocate for others' hair care.

This book will inspire and empower women of all races and backgrounds to learn that their femininity can be an adventure of beauty, confidence, and power; to value who they are, whether they have short or long hair or no hair, that their character and personality brings out their true beauty.

By the way, after completing this book, I discovered I the author, am *Dashing Dazzle*. So in this life time, I will continue to help women love the inner beauty of their character, as well as their outer beauty, as I will share knowledge of cherishing one's femininity, as I will also gift away beautiful wigs, in this lifetime, as one of the super powers, I possess to continue to empower women and girls all over the world, no matter what texture or differences of hair, to always value their own beauty.

Made in the USA
Monee, IL
08 June 2024